Six-Month Horse

Island Series • Prequel

Tudor Robins

Tudor Robins
www.tudorrobins.com

Publisher's Note: This is a work of fiction. Names, characters, places, and incidents are a product of the author's imagination. Locales and public names are sometimes used for atmospheric purposes. Any resemblance to actual people, living or dead, or to businesses, companies, events, institutions, or locales is completely coincidental.

Book Layout © 2017 BookDesignTemplates.com

Six-Month Horse/ Tudor Robins -- 1st ed.
ISBN 978-0-9958887-8-4 (paperback)
ISBN 978-1-990802-00-3 (hardcover)
ISBN 978-1-990802-13-3 (dust-jacketed hardcover)

Other Books by Tudor Robins:

Island Series:
Six-Month Horse (Prequel)
Wednesday Riders (Book Two)
Join Up (Book Three)
Faults (Book Four)
Reason Why (Book Five)

Stonegate Series:
Objects in Mirror (Book One)
After Lucas (Book Two)
Throw Your Heart Over (Book Three)

Perryside Series:
Moving North (Book One)

Mystery Stables:
Stolen Saddles (Book One)

Stand-Alones:
Meant to Be (Young Adult)
Before & After (Women's Fiction)
In Search Of (Small-Town Romance)

Chapter One

I come home dirty and tired.

Usually, when Slate stops on the way home from the barn to put gas in the car, and I use the gas station squeegee to wash the country dust off the windshield, I feel special as I stride around the car wearing my breeches and my tall black boots.

I get looks from other drivers and I think, *Yes, I've been riding a horse and I am lucky.*

Today I just felt grungy, and gross.

As I step inside the front hall, the huge, chunky-framed mirror my always-put-together mother loves so much shows me hair that's flat on top and flyaway on the sides, a shirt so far gone from its original white that it blends blandly with my beige breeches, and a face shining (not glowing) from today's unseasonable warmth.

The heat is also responsible for my wet armpits which just feel clammy now that I'm in the cool house.

"How was it?" My mom's voice floats from somewhere in the direction of the kitchen.

I'm not surprised my mom's home, but I am surprised she's not on the phone with a client from another time zone.

"It was fine." It's the best word to use for how I'm feeling right now. Not overly enthused about the ride I just had, and not prepared to get into the discussion it will prompt if I'm more honest and say it was "meh" or "not great."

I shouldn't have stayed up so late working on that essay last night.

The riding I'm doing is good for me. It's great experience. I mean, really, when I can get in a dozen rides a week – some of them on incredibly high-calibre horses – and I get paid, instead of forking out money for board and vet bills; well, it kind of makes the idea of paying to have my own horse seem crazy.

Right?

I just need to go to bed early tonight, then I'll feel better.

I lose my balance as I try to yank my foot free of my paddock boot and fall forward against the mirror. Even though the glass is cool and smooth under the hot skin of my forehead I can't stay like this. For one thing my mom will kill me if she sees the smudge on her spotless mirror. Also, it makes me look into my own eyes and see the weariness there.

This was one of my evenings for riding Charisma. He's beautifully bred, trained to the hilt, and is owned by a lady who just wants to win ribbons on him on the weekends. She pays me to keep him fit during the week and everyone at the barn keeps reminding me how lucky, lucky, lucky I am ... It's too bad he bores me stiff.

I went straight from boring to brazen when I got up on Peanut – a foul-tempered, wall-eyed, stout-legged paint, with a bad attitude and a big buck. Last week he dumped three lesson kids, which was Craig's cue to leave a note for me to climb up on him and teach him a lesson. Peanut gave me his customary fifteen minutes of fight, followed by an "OK, OK, I'll behave ..." capitulation. He'll be fine for a few weeks now, then he'll start bucking kids off again and I'll have to climb back up and press his reset button.

When I was twelve, wearing a pink I Love Horses t-shirt – the kind with hearts for the "o"s – I would have died to have an evening of riding like I just had.

Now I push away from the mirror, bend to yank the stubborn boot off, and entertain the thought of skipping riding tomorrow.

I'll get my energy back if I just eat some dinner.

Or should I shower first? I'm standing in my sweaty socks, making foggy marks on the shiny hardwood in the hall, completely unable to decide whether to head upstairs, or straight ahead into the kitchen, when my mom comes into the foyer, "Meg! You'll never guess who I've just been talking to on the phone."

The Attorney-General of Venezuela. No, wait, the Venezuela deal was last year. *The trade ambassador to the Hebrides.* Wrong time zone. The most logical guess would be Emily, my mom's long-suffering, always-available executive assistant, but Emily would never merit a *"you will never guess ..."*

My hesitation should give my mom the opening to say, 'Meg! *What have I told you about leaving footprints all over the clean floors?* but she doesn't say that. She doesn't even say, *'Well?'* and tap her foot for an answer from me. She just takes a breath and says, "Julie Czerny, that's who!"

Julie Czerny. My mom's right – I would never have guessed Julie Czerny, because I have no idea who she is.

"You remember, Meg. I went to law school with Julie. Only she never finished her articling because she met Peter Finley."

I do recognize Peter Finley's name. *Just.* "The hockey player?"

My mom nods. "*Ex* hockey player. Retired a couple of years ago and now he heads up scouting for some team or another." I stifle a smile. That my "i"s-dotted, "t"s-crossed mother, can't come up with the name of the team Peter Finley scouts for, shows that she's no more into hockey than I am.

My stomach rumbles and reminds me I'm hungry and I open my mouth to ask what ex-university class-mates, and ex-hockey players have to do with me, and my mom cuts me off at the pass by saying, "Come into the kitchen and you can have some of the soup I warmed up for dinner, while I tell you the rest."

The soup actually does smell quite good. I pad behind her, leaving more faint damp footprints on the floor, and the fact that she still says nothing says a lot about where her focus is right now. I climb up onto the stool in front of the kitchen island, accept a bowl of soup, and prepare to hear my mother out.

"Their daughter rides a horse." It takes me a second to realize we're talking about the aforementioned Julie Czerny and Peter Finley's daughter.

"Uh-huh." I swallow a mouthful of leeky, potatoey, cheesy, soup. Very yummy.

"Royal Highness – have you heard of him?"

Oh. That *horse.* An image of him jumps into my head fully-formed. Immaculate is the word that comes to mind when I think of him. Braids always neat and even, tack gleaming, boots spotless, tail flowing – perfectly complementing the shiny ribbons he always wins with his smooth strides, rock solid lead changes, and clean jumps.

"Big grey," I say to my mom. "Warmblood. Won two divisions at Champs last year." What I don't say is now I also have a picture of Vanessa Finley in my head. White breeches invariably Javex clean. Boots so shiny you could use their reflection to fix your hair. Always wearing jewellery – tasteful and expensive – the kind I would be terrified to wear because at the end of the day I'd have only one diamond-studded stirrup left in my earlobes, and I'd have lost half the charms off my silver bracelet.

"He's for lease," my mom says.

So, *this* is what the NHL player and his hockey wife have to do with me.

"Their daughter's been accepted to an equestrian boarding school in New Hampshire and she has a young new horse from Europe she'll be taking with her. They don't want to sell Royal – they want to make sure he retires with them – but he has a couple of good years of showing left in him and they'll lease him to the right rider."

Me. The daughter of the ex-university classmate. I can lease Royal if I want to.

My mom's been talking fast, tapping her toes, and twirling her pen through her fingers the way I've seen her do so many times before when she's in the process of closing a big deal. Clearly the Royal deal is one she'd like to seal for me.

Our family is financially secure. We have a nice house and there's money for me and my brother to go to university – that's a priority. But my disciplined parents will only spend so much on what they consider to be life's "extras." In fact, they'll argue the reason we are financially secure is precisely because they're careful with money.

We only have one car, and it isn't a luxury model. I have a sufficient clothing allowance to keep me decent, warm, and dry – anything more and I make up the difference. They'll pay for me to ride – the way they paid for my brother to swim competitively – but if I want to own a horse the purchase price is coming out of my savings.

So, this Royal opportunity presents the dream scenario, doesn't it?

A horse far, far out of my meagre price range. A horse guaranteed to take my show career to levels I could never have imagined. A horse I can ride for a couple of years, which brings me right up to when I'll be going to university and may not have time for a horse anymore, and a horse with a guaranteed wonderful retirement plan built right in.

I know it's perfect. Six months ago ... three months ago ... not long ago I would have been saying, "When can I try him?" and "I'm going to call Craig right now!" and I would have already texted Slate.

My mom's phone rings and I'm relieved because a) it's weird to have her undivided attention for so long and b) her answering it gives me time to sip at my soup – which is truly, very nice – and remind myself what a lucky person I am – one of the world's luckiest – and think about this opportunity that's more than golden, more than platinum, that's truly *Royal* ... and pinch myself because still, all I can feel is the same slightly fatigued, flat, bleakness I've been carrying with me all night, and – to be honest – for the last month.

To be precise, it'll be one month tomorrow. I've been both keeping track, and trying not to, of the time that's passed since I got the phone call. Craig's voice on the phone. Scary in itself because he never calls me. The knots in my stomach tightening when he asked, "How are you, Meg?" – not something Craig ever worries about. "It's not good news, I'm afraid," he said, and even though I already knew that, the knots in my gut all undid at the same time leaving my insides loose and liquid and making me sure I was about to be sick. "He didn't pass the vet check."

I knew it.

Which of course, was untrue. I *feared* it. Desperately.

We'd spent months, and months, and months, searching for a horse to fit my minimal budget, and the combined demands and expectations of my parents (who have a say because they'll pay for board), and Craig, and even me. I'd been shown a horse with one eye, and another missing an ear, there was one I'd had to wade out in mud over my boots to catch, and two who bucked me off – I'm pretty sure I was the first person to back them.

Then we'd found one. "Goody" was his barn name. "Too good to be true," I'd muttered under my breath. I could afford him – just. He had all his body parts. He was young and green – he had potential, but his owner had begun to develop that potential just enough so you could see where it could go. Which was out of sight. Sky's the limit. And – not that it really mattered to me anymore – he was a pretty horse, too.

I tried not to fall in love with him that first day because those words kept spooling through my head like a CNN ticker – *too good to be true, too good to be true* – but it was hopeless. He was a star all through his two-week trial at Craig's. The barn staff fell in love with him because he peed and pooped all in one corner. I fell in love with him as, with much snorting and head-turning, he discovered his own reflection in the mirrors in the indoor arena.

Turned out the day for Goody's vet check was one when I was stuck at school for a unit test in Math. "It'll be fine," Craig said. "We haven't seen a hint of anything wrong." *I don't know*, I thought. *Too good to be true.*

And I was right. And it hurt. And after I got off the phone with Craig I took myself and my dry-heaving stomach to hang over the toilet bowl, where I got to watch my tears splatting overlapping concentric rings in the still water.

"I think I'm done," I'd said to Craig, to my parents, to myself. My story was: "I'm going to university in a couple of years, anyway. I'd just find a horse and have to sell it again." The truth was: *I can't go through that again.*

Craig had taken the lemons of losing my sales commission and my future board, and made lemonade by using my experience to discipline his unruly schoolies, and offer me as a rider-for-hire to his boarders, which is how I got here, where I am, with my mother putting her phone down and saying, "Well?"

I look at her, and I don't know what to say. Which isn't going to go over well with my down-to-business, time-is-money parent.

I wait for a finger snap, a sigh, a follow-up, 'Come on, Meg!' and instead she presses her lips together and exhales, and says, "I know the disappointment with the chestnut was hard on you, Meg."

Even though she doesn't remember his name it's a big step for her to even know what colour he was. It's a big step for her to be empathetic about something even I feel like I should be over by now.

I smooth my crumpled napkin. "It *was* a bit ..."

"That's why I think this would be so great!" Her eyes are shining. "Imagine showing a horse like that. And it wouldn't be such a big commitment as owning your own horse. He wouldn't break your heart because you'd know he was going back to them at the end of the lease."

How can I explain to my mom that as much as it hurt when Goody broke my heart, I'm not sure I want to invest a lot of time into a horse that could never break it? It sounds stupid even to me.

"Thanksgiving weekend's coming up," my mom's saying. "Your dad will have to work on Saturday but you and I could go ahead to see this horse; make it a little road trip. You could ride him and we could have lunch in Kingston – maybe with Cam – then your father could catch up with us and we could have a nice family holiday at the cottage."

My mom never gets this excited about things that don't involve work or redecorating the house. She likes that I ride – once I said I might try rugby and she went very pale – and she likes Craig, but that's never prompted her to really take an interest in any individual horse. And her committing to free up an entire day; considering that happens rarely-to-never, how can I say no?

I don't. I say yes. And surely, when I see this amazing horse, and get to ride him, and know he could be mine to show ... surely I'll feel the magic then.

Chapter Two

Due to a spectacular screw-up on Slate's time-table last year, she and I are in the same biology class this semester, despite her being a year ahead of me in school. After months of complaining about the guidance counsellor's incompetence, when she saw the match on our timetable she said, "All is forgiven. I'll never complain again. Things happen for a reason, and that ridiculous error obviously happened so you and I could be lab partners."

And we are.

We're in my kitchen, heads down over the diagram of our fetal pig dissection. Sipping hot chocolate with my best friend is a good way to get through biology. It does feel like this was meant to be.

It's cold outside – my shoes left dark patches as I crunched across the frosted white turf in the park on my way to school this morning – but our house is warm, with the furnace humming, the smell of dinner heating in the oven (lasagna – my dad's favourite), and the background noises of the old floorboards of our house creaking as my mom paces, while her voice murmurs directions to Emily.

Whenever we need a break from labeling the spleen, and the cecum, and the pancreas, Slate finds YouTube videos of Royal winning ... pretty much everything ... He *is* gorgeous. "That could be you, my friend." Slate's pointing to Vanessa Finley, perched like a feather over the super-horse's withers.

"Only if I shrunk half-a-foot and had plastic surgery on my nose, and learned to take care of my boots ... look at the shine on those babies ..."

"I wouldn't be your best friend if you had a nose like hers; all tiny and ski-jumpy."

I sigh. "Which is pretty much exactly the nose I always wanted when I was a little kid."

"You're over that now, though, right?"

I grin. "I've come to accept prominent and bumpy."

"No, no, no." Slate shakes her head. "Defined and distinct."

"Girls, how's it going over here?" My mom's still wearing her headset, but I'm assuming she's between calls.

Slate toggles from YouTube to Google docs. "Hi Mrs. Traherne. Very well, thank you."

My mom leans in to examine our drawing. "What is this?"

"Oh! That's the liver," Slate says.

My mom blinks twice, fast, and recoils slightly. "It's a fetal pig," I explain.

My mother has two smiles. Tight-lipped, controlled, polite – this is the one I see ninety per cent of the time. Very occasionally she lets out a full-on, uninhibited, pure joy smile where she shows teeth, and the muscles around her eyes lift. The smile she gives now is slightly wobbly. "I was never very good at Biology."

Weakness and my mom are not two things I ever think of together but, just for a second there's vulnerability in the air. She clears her throat. "That was Emily on the phone."

I refrain from saying, 'Of course,' and just nod, "Yes?"

"I'm going to have to fly to Vancouver tomorrow."

"OK," I say. My mom's travel stopped being a problem as soon as I became old enough to be trusted with a house key, and with pre-heating the oven for dinner.

She adjusts her headset, pulls at the collar of her shirt. "Unfortunately, I have meetings right through to the weekend. The first flight Emily can book me back on is Sunday morning."

It takes a second for me to zoom out from my immediate focus of today, and this lab report, and tomorrow's ride on Charisma, to the end of the week. To realizing this is the week leading up to the Thanksgiving long weekend.

Starting with the Saturday my mom had earmarked for our road trip. To see Royal. To jump start our family Thanksgiving weekend.

"That's OK." A long, long time ago I learned it was the right thing to say because nothing was going to change and having a temper tantrum only ratcheted up everybody's stress levels.

I mean, I was the one who was lacking enthusiasm to start with. It's true my YouTube viewing with Slate has made me curious to try this horse, but it's not enough to rock the boat. To have my mom slamming dishes around saying, "I already feel guilty enough, Meg," and "It's not like I enjoy flying halfway across the country." To have my dad walk in to tension central and ask, "What's going on here?" To receive his tired sideways look asking me why I can't just leave it.

So I leave it. Same result, less angst.

"I'll email Julie and ask if we can reschedule," my mom says. "They're boarding the horse at a farm down the road – maybe they're available later in the weekend …"

"I can take Meg," Slate says.

"What?" my mom asks before giving her shoulders a little shake and correcting. "Pardon me?"

"We're going to my aunt's – near Toronto – and we were going to have to take two cars anyway, because we're bringing my grandmother, so I can just go ahead in the morning with Meg, then continue on from there." Slate shrugs. "I'd like to see this horse anyway, and it would be fun for Meg and I to have a road trip."

Road trip. Those are the danger words. The ones that purse my mom's lips and straighten her spine. When she backed out of the road trip she promised me, she didn't expect Slate to offer me one instead.

My dad walks into the awkward silence of nobody responding to Slate's offer, and calls, "Hello everybody! What's going on here?"

***

"I think she should go." It's my dad. They've already fast-forwarded past my mom saying, "Couldn't you, maybe ..." and my dad cutting her off to say, "You know I can't get out of my viewings that day, just the same way you can't get out of your travel. And, besides, Slate has offered. It's a chance for Meg to spend time with her best friend. It's controlled independence. It's good for her."

I'm sitting at the top of the stairs, chin propped on my knees, eavesdropping with zero shame at all. The conversation is about me. I have the right to hear it.

"But, Joe ... Slate can be – I don't know – a bit *flighty*. And she hasn't had her G2 license for that long. And she just got that car – I don't know what her mother was thinking – I wouldn't be giving a seventeen-year-old a car."

"Emily, there's perception and there's reality. While it's true Slate isn't always overly serious, in reality she's never been anything but solid and reliable when it comes to her friendship with Meg. And they'll be driving in the daylight, and she'll drop Meg off at Cam's afterwards ... and *you* wanted her to see this horse."

No answer. Which means my mom doesn't have a good argument, but I can picture the I-still-don't-like-this look she's giving my dad.

"And," he continues. "I'll give Meg and Cam a talk. I'll make our expectations clear."

"I still don't like it ..."

"I know this deal's been hard on you, Emily. You need a break. Go to Vancouver, get your work done, let me worry about things here, and you can meet us in Kingston on Sunday and we'll have that family Thanksgiving holiday you've been wanting so badly, even if it is a little shorter than expected."

"With turkey?"

"You don't like turkey."

"No, but it's not Thanksgiving without turkey."

"I'll pick you up at the train station in Kingston, and drive you to the grocery store and we'll buy every single thing we need for a turkey dinner and we'll take it to the island and cook it together at the cottage and you can make the kids peel the potatoes so it's a true family meal."

"Promise?" she asks.

"Promise. I'll tell them that's part of the deal when I talk to them."

She doesn't say OK, but I know I'm going. I tiptoe back to my room and email Slate, "Road trip's on ..."

As I'm saving our lab report and exiting from Google docs, her reply comes back. "Awesome bestie. Can't wait!"

Chapter Three

It rains Wednesday – one of those full-on cold autumn rains that makes me long for January when, sure, it's going to be cold, but it'll be bright, and sunny, and dry.

I'm soaked in the quick sprint from Slate's car to my front door, and the moisture turns the horse hair and dirt coating my skin to a brownish slime.

Not attractive. Straight into the shower.

I'm wrapping my hair in a towel when my dad taps on the door. "My office. As soon as you're decent."

When I get there, he's got the phone on speaker and is already talking. "Meg just walked in."

"Hey, Sis."

"Hey, Cam," I answer.

My mind flicks back to that conversation I overheard between my parents. "I'll give Meg and Cam a talk."

This is clearly the talk.

"So, Meg, Cam knows Slate's going to drop you off at his place Saturday afternoon. He'll be expecting you. Is that right, Cam?"

"Yup. Definitely. Expecting you, Sis."

"I'll send money with Meg. You two can go out to eat if you want. You can buy food for breakfast. Whatever you want. Your mother's going to take the red-eye to Toronto, then the train to Kingston so I'll pick her up from the train station on Sunday just before noon, then we'll come and get you two, and we're all going to go buy groceries for a turkey dinner and cook it together."

I know. I stop myself from saying it just in time, and say, "OK."

"Any questions?" my dad asks.

"No." My brother and I answer together.

"Now, here's the thing." My dad leans back in his chair and, even though Cam can't see him, I bet he knows my dad's doing it. There's a change in the tone of my dad's voice that says, *this is the part you really have to listen to.*

"Your mom is stressed. This deal is going on longer, and it's a lot tougher than she ever expected. She's got her heart set on a family Thanksgiving, and we're going to give it to her. Do you understand?"

What I hear when he says this is 'Don't screw this up, Cam. No last-minute drama. No mess-ups. Behave.'

I wonder if that's what my brother hears.

I wonder if my brother hears a message directed at me. Something like, 'Cut your mom some slack, Meg. Show some engagement – or at least some sympathy –

when she talks about her work. Be grateful when she shows an interest in your riding.'

My dad continues. "I'm not going to say much more, other than you're both smart and I know you can do this; that's the positive message. As for the negative message; if you don't – if you cause your mother stress – that will also cause me stress, and I'll make sure the stress trickles downhill right into both of your lives. Understood?"

Oh, I understand, alright. I translate the message to *'Cam, try not to screw up. Meg, if he does, you need to fix it.'*

"Yeah, Dad," I say.

"Of course, Dad," Cam says.

"Understood," we both say.

"Good," my dad says. "Then enjoy hanging out together on Saturday, and get ready to be the happiest of happy families starting Sunday."

Chapter Four

The scenery flips by – tree, tree, tree, lake, island, lake, field ... Lots of cows. One place with alpacas. A couple with horses.

We've had cold days already – frost more than once – which is why the mildness of this Thanksgiving weekend comes as a gift. The sun beaming through the windshield washes my face, warms my bones. My body is loose and lazy in the passenger seat.

But it doesn't last long.

A sign looms up displaying the Provincial Park logo and showing a right-turn arrow at the exact same time as the GPS lady on Slate's phone says, "Prepare to turn right in two-hundred metres."

This is good. The barn is in the middle of nowhere, but it's in the middle of nowhere next to a middle-of-nowhere park I've actually been to once before, back in my Girl Guide phase. We spent two days tramping around in the rain, hiking until all of us had raw spots rubbed on our feet, walking farther than I've ever walked before – while wearing a loaded backpack – and when our leader showed us how much of the park territory we covered, it was a mere sliver.

"Blister Park," I say.

Of course, it's not really called Blister Park, but Slate knows the story. She shakes her head. "You used to bug me to join Guides with you, but who was the smart one?"

"Well, the silver lining of that long-ago trip is that I now know we're definitely going in the right direction."

"Hmm ..." Slate says. "Seems like a long time to wait for a pay-off." She slows and negotiates the signposted turn. "So, you excited?"

"Good question," I say. "I should be, shouldn't I?"

"I mean, it's amazingly cool just to get to ride him," Slate says.

"Yeah, you're right." She *is* right. That's a good way to look at it. No matter what happens, today I get to ride a truly accomplished, talented horse at the top of his game. That's a privilege. "Thanks," I tell her.

"Thanks for driving you to the middle of nowhere?" As though prompted, the disembodied GPS voice guides us off the crumbling-but-paved road we've been on, onto a much-narrower gravel track.

"I know. I can't believe Slate Rochefort, city-girl extraordinaire is out here in the back of beyond with me."

She takes a hand off the steering wheel long enough to pat my knee. "Well, you're my bestie, Meg."

"Aww ..." Even if riding hasn't brought me the horse of my dreams – yet – it brings me time with Slate.

She grips the steering wheel tightly as her little car rattles over a course of bumps, then adds, "And I want you to have a horse you love as much as I love Obsidian."

"Or at least one with both ears."

She giggles. "Totes right. Two ears would be the bomb."

***

Ears, of course, are not a problem. Royal has two perfectly formed ones that show his alertness and intelligence as they swivel to catch a chickadee call from outside, the rustle-bustle of another horse shifting in his stall further back in the barn, and me saying, "Hey, handsome. Nice to meet you."

Heather, the barn owner / manager, surprises me. She's so young I feel like she should be in university; not living in a farmhouse with no neighbours within sight, responsible for acres and acres of land and – from a quick glance at the barn and surrounding paddocks – quite a few horses.

As she leads us toward the barn Slate bumps me and mutters, "Do you think she's in the witness protection program? Or in hiding after carrying out a horrific crime?"

"Shh ...!" I love Slate, but she's full of opinions and she only thinks she's good at hiding them. "What are you talking about, anyway? Why would you say that?"

"Look at her! She's really cute – hot, even – and young, and she lives out here ..." Slate flings her arms wide to the graveled yard where we parked – the wind cartwheeling dried leaves across it in a northern version of tumbleweed – and the fields beyond; summer green being edged out by autumn-gold fall grasses.

It looks pretty good to me, but this isn't a debate I'm about to get into with Slate. My best friend and I have already established we won't be going to the same university. She wants bright-lights-big-city, and I want small-town-homey. Part of me thinks if it wouldn't result in me being excommunicated from my family I'd skip higher education altogether and settle somewhere just like this.

Reaching the barn lets both of us turn our attention to Heather. "I'm so glad you could come. I know it was a long drive, but I think you'll find this guy is worth it. It's a privilege to look after him for the Finleys while they're away in Europe – he's a perfect gentleman – no vices at all."

"He's so clean." I walk all around the big, strong gelding without seeing a single mark on his flea-bitten grey coat. "I hope you didn't bathe him for us. We're not that picky."

Heather shakes her head. "No, like I said, he's a dream to look after. One of those rare greys who keeps himself clean. I have yet to see a manure stain on his coat."

"Tick," Slate says, and I know what she means. When we tried to make a list of pros and cons for this horse, it was hard to come up with too many cons, but one of them was keeping his light coat clean – "There's a reason I own a near-black horse," Slate said. Now, apparently, we can cross that potential problem off the list.

"Well," Heather says. "Mrs. Czerny said she's happy for you to put this guy through his paces so you can make sure you like him. Do you want to get on him?"

I take a second too long to answer, and Slate says, "Well if you don't, I'm going to. Have you seen his saddle? It's worth more than my first pony was."

Once again she's right – about the horse and the saddle – I'm about to have one of the best rides of my life. Time to mount up.

* * *

Heather wasn't lying about Royal's manners. When I lead him to the ring, the big horse walks forward, without rushing me, right at my shoulder. He stands stock-still while I mount, and waits patiently while I adjust my stirrups and double-check the girth.

I'm used to horses that test, and push – that see what they can get away with and only behave once I make it clear I'm going to make them. This horse starts from a default position of politeness. It's lovely. It's easy. I can see how people would get used to it.

"Nice manners," Slate says.

"No doubt," I answer.

Heather smiles, but she doesn't know the underlying conversation Slate and I are having. *Too perfect?* I'm wondering, and *Wait and see,* my friend is cautioning.

Royal's walk is long and eager and he frames himself up before I even lift the reins. When I do take contact, his mouth is soft and steady.

Most horses I ride either charge off with their own agenda in mind, or are tentative until they're told what to do.

This horse moves forward with confidence, but always has one ear turned toward me. I feel like he's saying, 'I'm just going to go ahead and get us moving, but you let me know as soon as you want to do something and I'm all good with that.'

Which is true. All I have to do is turn my head and he moves into a round, twenty-metre circle. I look inward and he spirals it down to ten metres.

Back on the rail, I think *trot* and he trots. This is the first thing I could imagine somebody faulting this horse on – his stride is so powerful I struggle to get my seat back into the saddle between posting – but, really, the weakness isn't in him, it would be in any rider who couldn't handle his incredible strength.

He serpentines, leg yields, and shortens and lengthens over trot poles.

In his canter comes the pay-off for his explosive trot, because the three-beat stride is glass-smooth – as easy to sit as an armchair.

Transitions don't phase him – he pops up and down every ten strides, five strides, three strides, never running into his new stride. His lead changes are seamless. I'm not always sure he's done them, except Slate says, "Yup," "Nice," and, more than once, "Tick!"

I've worked the gelding fairly hard, and with Vanessa away, I can't imagine he's been ridden that much lately, but even under the unseasonably warm sun, Royal hasn't broken a sweat.

"He's fit," I tell Heather.

She nods. "He's very strong. It was a long show season, but as you can see it didn't wear him down. He responds well to hard work."

I lift my eyebrows at Slate, and she mouths, *Careful*.

It's not fair to dislike this horse because he's perfect. What kind of person would do that?

I'm doing it.

"Do you want to jump him?" Heather asks.

A massive weariness washes through me. I know how he'll jump. There won't be any surprises. He'll pick an excellent spot. He'll lift with smooth power. He'll clear the jump by half-a-foot at least. I won't have to do anything.

On the one hand, of course anyone would want to jump a horse like that. On the other hand ... what's the point?

"Yes, please," Slate says, and I love that even if Slate doesn't always know what she *shouldn't* say, she definitely knows what I should.

Heather steps into the ring to set up a couple of jumps and I walk Royal in lovely figures-of-eight and stroke his neck and tell him he's a very, very good and handsome and lovely boy. And in my head, I know everything I'm saying is true.

***

Slate and I have spread our lunch out across a picnic table under a maple tree that occasionally swirls big leaves into the middle of our spread of sandwiches and veggies and dip. Royal has been turned out in a paddock abutting the barn and, while I chew, I watch him graze and stroll, and enjoy the strength of the sun on his back.

"So," Slate says.

"So," I answer.

"Was he as good as you thought he'd be?"

"Probably better. He makes Charisma feel like a cart horse."

She takes a bite of a carrot. "How about I tell you what I saw?"

That sounds good. Slate talking so I don't have to think. "Sure. Go for it."

"I saw a really, truly, beautiful horse."

I nod.

"I saw some nice riding from you – not a piano hand in sight."

I grin. "And that is a real accomplishment for me."

"I saw an opportunity for you to go to shows you never thought you could, and to win ribbons at those shows ..."

I take a deep breath. Wait for her to tell me not to waste time, to suck it up, say "yes please" and text my mom to send an eTransfer to her university friend.

"... and I saw no chemistry at all."

Oh. I exhale pent-up worry and tension I didn't know I was holding. I'm not crazy. Or at least, if I am, I'm not the only crazy person in the world. Slate is also nuts.

She looks at me, lifts her eyebrows. "So?"

"Thank you," I say. What I don't say is, *That's why you're my best friend.* Because she gets it. She knows me. And I don't have to say that to her because she already knows.

The relief makes me push away from the picnic table and spin around in the sunny clearing and, when I notice Royal watching me, walk over to his paddock to slip him a carrot. "You are such a lovely boy."

The only problem is, the minute I come back, and drop back into my seat across from Slate, the lightness flees. "This pretty much confirms it, though, right? If I can't fall for this horse, I'm never going to find one, am I?"

Slate tilts her head to the side. "OK, so the 'no chemistry' thing. That's just a fact. It's not a conclusion."

I pull my eyebrows together. "What do you mean?"

"I mean, not everyone experiences love at first sight. Hannah Gillespie said she never wanted a mare, and especially not a chestnut ..."

"... and she's showing her chestnut mare in Florida this winter," I finish.

"You got it."

"So, you're saying ... what, exactly?"

"I'm saying maybe you have to decide whether you want a great horse, right away, or whether you want to fall head over heels, which might happen ... who knows when? And this horse isn't a huge commitment. You can lease him for a couple of years, you can treat each other well, and – let's face it – you'll probably end up loving him at least a little bit."

"Is that what you'd do?" I ask.

Slate shrugs. "I'm really sorry, but I can't answer that. I don't have to make that decision. I'm just laying out the options." It's her turn to lever herself out of the restrictive picnic table bench. "And now, I'm going to find a bathroom – preferably one with actual heat and plumbing, if such a thing exists out here."

"Slate?"

"Yeah?"

"Please don't say that to Heather when you ask her where the bathroom is."

She claps her hand over her breastbone. "Meg! I'm offended. Don't you think I know my manners?"

"Oh, I'm pretty sure you *know* them ... I'm just not always sure you *use* them."

She grins. "I'll behave. See you in a few."

I swirl some hummus onto a carrot stick and prop my chin on my hand as I gaze toward Royal's paddock. He is so, so lovely, and secure, and stable. I do this thing sometimes, where I imagine horses as people. In that scenario Royal is the most popular guy at school, but not the captain-of-the-football-team, get-drunk-every-Friday-night, ask-you-on-a-date-and-tell-you-to-meet-him-inside-the-movie-theatre-so-he-doesn't-have-to-pay-for-your-ticket kind of popular. Instead he's the guy that literally everybody in the school likes. All the staff and teachers know his name because it's on the honour roll every year, sporty guys like him because he's an athletic god, every other student likes him because he's kind and will always share his notes, and when his parents let him use the car he brings it back with the gas tank full.

Putting it that way, it would be a huge mistake to let this horse slip out of my grasp.

There's a tickle at the back of my neck – something trailing across my skin – Slate isn't the sneak-up-behind-and-yell-"Guess who?" type, but there's a first for everything. "Slate?"

The tickle drags back the other direction across my neck. "OK, Slate, that's just creepy ..."

I turn around to look right up a huge nostril.

A huge, hairy nostril. With juicy snot droplets in it.

"Oh!" While this is a stable, and I expect there to be horses, I don't expect them to sneak up behind me in a non-fenced area while I'm eating my lunch.

While I'm off guard the horse reaches his nose over my shoulder and stretches his dexterous lip toward the carrot sticks left in the middle of the table. The weight of his neck pushes on my shoulder, pinning me to my seat.

"Whoa, whoa, whoa ..." There's clearly only one way I'm going to get him to back off. I shoot my free hand out and scoop up the carrots. He snorts and lifts his head.

"I know," I say. "I'm so mean, aren't I? But, seriously, dude – that was super-rude."

Now that I'm free to move I swing my legs around so I'm facing out on the bench. The horse has taken one step back, but he's still watching me.

"Here," I put my hands together to form a shallow cup containing all the remaining carrot sticks. "Go crazy."

He does, but first he blows long and hard through his nostrils and all those snot droplets I saw spray all over my arms.

"Thank you so much," I say.

His ears flick toward me and he blinks. I think he's saying *No problem*. What he's probably saying is, 'Is that all? No more carrots?'

He's got a whorl exactly in the middle of the space between his eyes. With the carrots gone, I reach my fingers up to scratch that whorl. For some horses, this would be the end. Do. Not. Touch. My. Face. He not only lets me dig my fingernails into the coarse hair, he closes his eyes, and pushes against them, and sighs.

Deep inside me something goes click.

I've felt this before. Once before. I was four, and scared. My mom had dropped me off for my first day of junior kindergarten and I was wearing a uniform made of wool that itched my skin, and the classroom had a sharp smell that hurt my nose and, as far as I could tell through my surreptitious, don't-make-eye-contact glances, none of the other little girls looked like they were about to cry.

Meanwhile I was sniffing so hard I was afraid I was going to get a nosebleed, and I had tears rising, hot and ready, toward the spilling point.

The woman's face, when she knelt in front of me, was blurred by my watery vision, and while I was blinking she put her hand on my arm and said, "My little girl is lonely, too. Would you like to be her friend?" and with those words something inside me ticked over, and a smile chased away my tears and even though Slate was a year older, and we ultimately ended up in different kindergarten classes, Slate's mother's words bonded me to her daughter for life.

This feels the same as that, and look how the Slate thing turned out.

"Hey Buddy," I say. "Let's go find out who you are."

Chapter Five

The thing is, the horse isn't wearing a halter.

And, despite Craig's constant drilling that a belt is an integral part of a well-turned-out rider's wardrobe, I'm not wearing one.

I rise from the bench and the horse lifts his head a couple of inches and watches me.

"What are we going to do with you?"

I take a couple of steps and he slowly, calmly, steps with me.

I stop and he stops.

"Well, OK," I say. "Let's go find Heather."

I walk across the lawn, onto the graveled area in front of the barn and the horse walks beside me. We pass a horse trailer, with a cat sunning itself on the running board. The horse snorts at the cat, who gives him a warning hiss, but he stays by my side.

He's tall. I gauge his sharp withers in relation to my own height and peg him at around 16.3.

His legs are disproportionately long. I don't have to bend down far to look right under his belly. Except, when I do that he stops and tries to circle around me. I straighten again. "No, no ... we're going this way."

He snorts in a, *I'm-not-the-one-who-stopped* kind of way.

He's a very dark bay showing too many ribs and too few dapples. In fact, there's nothing dappled about his ragged coat, punctuated with old, tough-looking scars and a couple of fresh cuts. The scratches don't look serious, but they also don't look pretty.

I lean into the barn but the inside is dim after the bright autumn sunshine outside, and because the far doors are also open, the light that washes in through them puts the middle aisle and stalls into grainy shadow. "Heather? Are you here?"

The horse bumps my back.

No answer from Heather.

"Well, we'll just have to keep looking."

It's only as I'm turning, with the horse still glued to my side, that I realize I could have found a halter and / or a lead rope in the barn. I shrug. He's showing no signs of leaving me, so I guess we're doing fine.

Voices drift to me and I see Heather and Slate strolling along the drive from the house to the barn.

I snap my fingers – "This way!" and the horse and I wander over to meet them.

Heather and Slate stop and watch us approach, and when we reach them the horse gives me a quick sniff, then drops his nose to the long grass growing at the side of the drive and begins munching.

"Well, well, well – who do we have here?" Slate asks. I'm watching the hollows above the horse's eyes dip and rise as he chews, and I lift my eyes to hers when she asks the question. "*Oh ...*" she says. And nods. "I see. It's like that."

Meanwhile Heather's oblivious to the obscure continuation of our conversation from earlier. "Oh no, Pearl again ..." she says.

"His name's Pearl?" I take a step back and look the horse over tip to tail. There's no accounting for naming conventions, especially with thoroughbreds, but he doesn't look like a Pearl.

She shakes her head. "Sorry. No. Not him. Pearl is our neighbour down that way." She waves to the west. "I've been turning this guy out with Pearl's pony, Millie. The problem is, when Pearl visits Millie, she doesn't always close the gate behind her. This is the third time I've found this guy out wandering on his own. It'll be a miracle if I don't lose him before he ships out on Tuesday."

"This coming Tuesday?" I ask.

"Mm-hmm," she says. "He's here in transit from a racetrack in New York. My friend who runs a trail riding barn near Sudbury saw him on a racehorse rescue organization she follows on Facebook and agreed to take him. She found someone to haul him this far and I'm keeping him here for a few days until she can get him the rest of the way. Anyway, I'd better find a halter and get him safely behind a closed gate ..."

She's already walking toward the barn and calls over her shoulder, "I'll be right back if you don't mind waiting with him."

"No! I don't mind at all!" I turn back to face Slate who has both hands clasped over her heart. "Ha! Leave you alone for two seconds and you go fall in love behind my back."

"Guilty," I say. "Do you think she'll let me ride him?"

"You can ask."

So, when Heather comes back, I do.

"Oh ..." she says. "I don't know the last time he was ridden, or if he even has been since leaving the track."

"That's OK. I've ridden lots of youngsters, and greenies. I'm fine to ride him."

She's shaking her head. "I wouldn't feel comfortable with it. I have no idea what to expect from him – I don't even have tack for him – and, I mean, you came here to ride *Royal*." She says it like I've just asked to ride a donkey and it's her job to remind me I was looking for a horse – that's how different these two creatures are.

I get where Heather's coming from. I can see how, to her, my request is coming totally out of left field. Even though I'm the one who'll ride, and show, the horse, Heather's loyalty isn't to me at all. It's to her neighbour clients – the Czerny / Finley family – and to my mom, who arranged this meeting, and probably also to Craig who was copied on all the emails. Craig runs an active show barn with lots of clients always looking for new horses. Someone just starting out, with a small barn, like Heather would want to stay on the good side of Craig – might hope to sell a horse now and then to one of his fairly wealthy students – and we both know Craig would definitely not be happy if today's trip resulted in me bringing home this horse instead of Royal.

"Here's the thing," I say. "I understand what you're saying. But there's something about this horse – I just need to know what he's like to ride."

I'm losing her. She's shaking her head. I rush to add, "And you're probably right – it will be a disaster, and a waste of all of our time – but at least I'll *know*, and I can move on and concentrate on Royal."

The horse lifts his head from the side-of-the-driveway grass and pokes me between the shoulder blades. I imagine he's reacting to me calling him a disaster. I try not to smile.

Heather sighs. "I get that you have a feeling about this horse. I respect it. But it really doesn't matter. Royal is available. This horse isn't. He's not mine to let you ride or not ride – much less buy. He belongs to my friend. So even if you rode him, nothing could come of it. Given that, it's not a risk I'm going to take."

I like Heather. Maybe I like her more than before. And I want to shake her.

The horse lifts his head again, and Heather wordlessly hands me the halter she's brought. He obligingly noses his face into it then he gives a long, rattling snort that flecks my breeches with sloppy bits of green grass, and lips all along my legs, as though trying to clean his mess. It makes me laugh, at first, until I become sure the laughter's going to turn to tears.

Slate catches me blinking hard through blurry eyes, and she turns to Heather. "Could you, maybe, just think about it? Could you call your friend and see if she'd really mind if Meg tried him? Maybe she'd be willing to take a quick profit on him and rescue another horse?"

"It's not about money," Heather says.

"That's pretty clear ..." Slate says.

I'm afraid she's going to make a comment about the state of whatever bathroom facilities she just used so I clear my throat and kick a stone in her direction.

"What I mean ..." Slate looks at me with both eyebrows arched toward her hairline. "... is that I've been helping Meg look for a horse for a long time. She's had a lot of disappointments and if she has a feeling about this one, I really wish she could at least try him. So, agreed, it's not about money, but if it came to that she'd pay your friend fairly for him."

Heather's cheeks are flushed. "I don't know what to say."

"Just please, please say you'll think about it," I say. "That's all. And if you decide I can try him, I'll come back. I'll figure out a way."

The horse head butts me and I twirl my fingers through his forelock.

"I'll think about it." Heather says.

Slate claps her hands together.

"I'll *think* about it. That's all."

"Thank you!" I say. "Thank you, thank you, thank you! If you change your mind you can text me. Like I told you earlier, I'm going to be on the island for Thanksgiving, and I don't always have good cell coverage, but messages do come through eventually, and if you text me I'll call you back."

Heather looks at the shaggy, bony horse beside her. "That feeling of yours must be a really strong one to keep you from saying yes to Royal right this second."

"The heart wants what it wants," Slate says.

I've heard that expression before, but I've never really understood it. Until now. Now I'm living it.

"One more thing ..." I say, and Heather bites her lip. "Don't worry! It's nothing huge. Just ... if he's not named Pearl, could you tell me his real name?"

She laughs. "I guess that's the least I can do. In fact, maybe it'll cure you of wanting him – his registered name is Major Disaster."

"Oh!" Maybe that's why he head-butted me when I said he'd probably be a disaster. At any rate, it's one more nail in the coffin of this horse. He'd never be allowed in Craig's barn with a name like that. Last year a girl brought in a horse called "Trouble at the Henhouse" and Craig made her rename him, "Ahead by a Century." No "Troubles" "Hazards" or "Dangers" allowed in Craig's barn. "Disaster" is a definite no-no.

"Still love him?" Slate asks.

I run my fingers along the crest of his neck. "Still love you, Major."

And that's the way I have to leave it.

* * *

"Sorry," Slate says as we buckle our seat belts. "I wish I'd been able to make a better argument."

"Don't be stupid. Number one: you didn't insult her."

Slate snorts. "As if I would have ever ..."

"Hmm ... anyway, most importantly, you made her think. You gave me a shot."

She turns the key in the ignition and says, "Well, now that I know his name, I really hope you get him. I'd love to see the look on Craig's face when you ship in a horse a couple of hundred pounds underweight, who looks like he's walked through a hall of knives, named Major Disaster."

She negotiates around a couple of big potholes and says, "Listen, to soothe your broken heart, how about we go to that super-amazing cupcake place in Kingston and ease your sorrows with sugar and butter?"

Before I can answer my phone buzzes.

I swipe the screen open. "Oh," I say.

"What?"

"It's my brother."

Slate lifts an eyebrow. "Why do I feel like cupcakes downtown just got pushed off the agenda?"

I sigh. "Well, downtown's still on the cards but maybe not-so-much cupcakes ..."

"OK, OK, speaking of Major Disasters, tell me which one your brother's gotten himself – and us – into now."

Chapter Six

If you cause your mother stress, that will also cause me stress, and I'll make sure the stress trickles downhill right into both of your lives.

One hundred per cent, no doubt about it, my brother being kicked out of his latest house is an all-round stress-causing event.

It's not even that I'm supposed to sleep there tonight, and that my parents are expecting to pick us both up there tomorrow morning – although, come to think of it, that's going to be a problem. It's more the speed and frequency with which my brother's cycled through university accommodation. He started early, getting kicked out of residence in first year for making money by sleeping at his girlfriend's house on the weekends while he rented his dorm room out on Airbnb.

"Remind me, how many houses is this?" Slate asks.

I shrug. "It would be safe to say he's had about three addresses a year."

"Is it always the sleeping-with-roommate-gone-bad thing?" Slate changes lanes, then adds, "Or, no, I remember one time it was sleeping-with-the-roommate's-girlfriend."

"I think that happened twice, but there was also that time he moved in with six engineers and the landlord took them to court for building a half-pipe in the living room."

"Oh lord, you're right. And your mother tried to represent them in small claims court, but she lost because your brother's defense was, 'I don't understand the problem. We boarded up the windows so nobody would crash through them.'" Slate shakes her head. "I still can't believe your mom took the day off work to even attend their case."

I nod. "I know, but I think that's the whole point. She was sure she could just swoop in there and win that case – then punish my brother in private, of course – and when it didn't work out that way my mom was angrier at my brother staining her reputation by making her lose a small claims court case than she was about the actual eviction."

"And loss of the damage deposit."

"That, too ..." Thinking of my mom's taken all the funny out of my back-and-forth reminiscences with Slate.

Cam's done it again. I should have known he would. Stirring the pot, rocking the boat, causing trouble ...

they're Cam's specialties and this time I'm going to get burned, too, just when I need my parents as happy as they can be.

Just when I need my mom enjoying the Thanksgiving of her dreams, receptive to my gentle suggestion that we just maybe, perhaps, consider not leasing the world-beating, perfectly mannered, top-of-his-game horse from her fellow university alum, and instead take a tiny little chance on a reasonably priced horse absolutely packed with potential.

That's how I was planning to present it to her, anyway. Preferably when she had a belly full of turkey and apple pie, and a glass of red wine in her hand.

Thanks a bunch, Cam.

***

Slate's gearing down to make the turn off the concession road, onto the two-lane highway toward the city. As she completes the turn, I say, "You know, you don't have to come at all. Even if I'm on the hook to help him because he's my brother, well, he's not your brother and this isn't what you signed up for today. You can just drive me to the first city bus stop then get on the highway."

"Mmm-hmm," she says. "That's probably what I'm going to do."

"Seriously, Slate."

"Seriously, Meg. You're my super-bestie so if you're on a hook, then I'm hanging right there with you."

"I'm lucky," I say. There are people in this world without enough food, without a place to live; who couldn't imagine having the choice between two horses as their main problem in life. Maybe "lucky" is wrong. Maybe "spoiled" would be more accurate.

"You are. We both are, but that doesn't mean you should just never fight for what you want – that you should never try to be happy – I'm pretty sure you not getting Major wouldn't solve all the rest of the world's problems."

"OK," I say, and sit back in the passenger seat and watch the tar-seamed bleached asphalt road spool beneath us. We mostly pass trees, or fenced pastures, but every now and then a driveway opens to a farmhouse. They're modern or old, well-kept or neglected. Their mailboxes tend to match them; some battered and leaning, others undented and upright. In the fields around the houses sit everything from the ancient square-logged, white-chinked barns so common in the east of the province, to hulking modern milking barns, and solar panels. Old and new farming, but definitely farm country.

I hug my luck tightly around me. To be here. To have beauty around me. To be with Slate. Then, for a second,

I let my thoughts tunnel in again. Back to the shaggy horse who sought me out. I press on the button that summons his memory. Yup. Still tender.

I make myself a promise that if ever, in any way, giving Major up will bring about something momentous – like world peace – I'll do it. But as long as that's not the case I'm going to try to figure out how to make that horse mine. And if digging my brother out of trouble helps me do it, well, I guess I'll get a shovel.

Two long, high ridges of layered limestone funnel us under an overpass – the overpass of the busiest highway in the country – and we hit instant city. Or, more correctly, instant congestion, drive-thrus, box stores, gas stations, traffic lights, and sidewalks with nobody walking on them.

A red light confronts us and we roll to a stop. "Do you know where we're going?" Slate asks.

"Head for the university," I say. "The exact address is somewhere in one of Cam's texts."

**

Turns out we don't need the address.

I know my way around the student housing area well enough to direct Slate to Cam's street, and once we're there, it's impossible to miss his house.

In a long line of buildings with unkempt yards – most having some amount of garbage, or discarded bikes, or tattered lawn furniture on them – the front lawn of my brother's as-of-now former home is covered with boxes and garbage bags with stuff spilling out of them. There's a futon. The yoga ball he uses as a desk chair is rolling back and forth in the breeze.

It should be a pathetic scene. Cam should look abandoned and more-than-a-little desperate. Obviously nobody's told him that, though.

As Slate snugs her car against the curb, Cam rises from the crumbling front steps with a huge grin on his face. "Hey, Sis! And Slate! So great to see you two." His tall frame is thinner than the last time I saw him. The lost weight makes his cheekbones pop, and his jeans hang off his hips in a coolly casual way. His smile brings creases to the skin around his mouth and eyes, and his too-long hair flops over his forehead. As always he's wearing one of what my dad calls his "jaunty hats" – Cam regularly finds, buys, and is gifted weird and wonderful tuques, and he has a way of wearing them that looks swank. On anybody else (me) they'd just look goofy.

The part of Slate that's like my brother – the magnetic, charismatic part – responds to him. She smiles, and lets him hug her and says, "Nice place you've got here, Cam. Or should I say, 'Nice place you had ...'" I never have to worry about Slate's bluntness with Cam. In fact, as far as I'm concerned, she can be as blunt as she likes.

Fire-coloured leaves spiral down from the massive maple tree overhead, landing softly on my brother's worldly goods, and he laughs and shrugs. "Oh well. I was going to have to move anyway when I go to Montreal."

And, with that, we're closing in on the reason my brother should want to stay on my parents' good side. His academic career, up until now, has been of the two-steps-forward-one-step-back variety. He's brilliant – that's undeniable. Professors note his brilliance and re-cruit him for their pet research projects. He joins, he excels ... until he doesn't. Until he gets bored; until he remembers this wasn't his pet project, and starts slack-ing off. Come to think of it, it's a bit the way he is with girlfriends, which probably explains why we're all stand-ing out here right now.

"So, I guess Lauren's not moving to Montreal with you," I say.

His eyes slide toward the house. "Hmm, yeah. The topic did come up."

While Cam was home this summer he told me about a research project he wants to work on. "Look at this, Sis," he said, and clicked me through the website and even though I have no particular interest in marine biology, it looked cool enough that I can see why he wants to go.

Roadblock one: It means switching schools – away from my parents' alma mater – a school they're both insanely and – in my opinion – irrationally, attached to.

Roadblock two: Because of Cam's up-and-down transcript he's confident he can get the department to accept him, but it's unlikely they'll give him funding.

My brother likes being a student, but I'm pretty sure he has no desire to be a starving student and my dad's words are still there, right at the surface of my brain – I'll make sure the stress trickles downhill right into both of your lives – I'm not sure why those words aren't terrifying my brother. If it was me, permanently locked out of the house my parents have been paying rent on, surrounded by boxes and bags of all the belongings they'd bought for me over the years, I'd be having kittens.

It's not me, though. It's Cam.

He rubs his hands together. "Well, onwards and upwards, right?"

"Onwards and upwards to where, exactly?" I ask.

"No time to explain now, Lauren said she was calling the landlord if I didn't have everything off the lawn in ..." Cam drops his eyes to his watch, "... about an hour. So, let's see how much of this we can shove into Slate's car, shall we?"

"Shall we Slate?" I ask.

"Of course we shall, Meg. What else would we do?"

"Aw, you two are the best," Cam says. "I'm going to see if I can figure out how to put this futon on the roof."

Chapter Seven

My brother knows a guy – a PhD student – who just got offered a late-term teaching assignment at another school in another city and is willing to sub-let Cam his apartment effective immediately. Cam can move his stuff into the garage for the weekend until they do the key handover.

This in no way surprises me. My brother is world-famous for landing on his feet. Growing up, if Cam skipped a class, the teacher would be away sick anyway. If he broke curfew, my parents were late getting home. Once he put a scratch on the car and before my parents could notice it, my mom got into a fender-bender at the grocery store that completely covered it up.

Meanwhile, one Christmas a client gave my mom a box of u(a)ber-expensive truffles made with white chocolate and macadamia nuts that had been through the digestive tract of a koala bear (or something like that). The chocolates disappeared from the drawer in Cam's old room where my mom had hidden them, and I got grounded. Even though I hate white chocolate. Even though my brother had been home earlier in the day to snag clean socks and underwear, which I wasn't allowed to tell anybody because he was only in town overnight to go to a concert with some friends, and he hadn't told my parents.

Slate's car is groaning with Cam's belongings, and there are still a couple of things that are going to require a second trip. Slate points to Cam. "There's only room for two of us in the car. You can walk over. We'll meet you there."

"But ..." he says. "I should go with you in the car. You won't be able to find the place without me. Meg can meet us there."

Slate puts a hand on her hip. "If Meg and I can't find it in the car, how is Meg supposed to be able to find it walking on her own?"

Cam grins. "It was worth a try." He touches his fingers to his forehead in a mock salute. "See you there."

The space left in the front seat for Slate and me feels like a cave, with the wall of Cam's belongings blocking out all light and sightlines from behind us.

"Thanks," I say.

"For what?"

"For putting my brother in his place. Which is walking."

"You just have to stand up to him, Meg. He's selfish, but he's not unreasonable. Cam starts from a place of taking whatever he can get away with ..." She smiles and says, "I know, because I'm the same way in my family." Then continues. "But if you push back he'll fall in line."

"I'm not good at that."

She nods. "Of course you aren't, because you've never seen anyone – *your parents* – do it. But that doesn't mean you can't start."

"Huh. I'll take it under advisement."

Slate turns the key in the ignition. "I'm always here for coaching if you need it."

As we roll away from the curb, a text buzzes in on her phone. "Check that, would you?"

"It's your mom. She wants to know if you're still on track to meet them at your aunt's by dinner."

"Text her back 'yes'."

I check the time on her phone, lift my eyebrows. "Doesn't your aunt live three hours away?"

"It's parental management, Meg. Either way, I'm going to be late for dinner."

"Um, like *way* late."

"Yeah, so at some point they're going to be stressed. This way, they can be relaxed for a couple of hours until they figure out I'm actually not arriving in time for dinner. Or, I can tell them the truth now and they'll be stressed the entire time."

"But Slate, that's ..."

"... classic Cam. I know. Like I said, in my family I'm a bit like Cam. But, you see, my heart is in the right place."

"I don't know how you can go through life taking stuff like this so lightly."

She laughs. "I don't know how *you* can go through life taking stuff like this so seriously. Honestly, Meg, you'll give yourself an aneurysm."

Easy for Slate to say. Her mom's nowhere near as tightly wound as mine. I turn in my seat to face her. "If you're so much like Cam, how come I love you so much?"

Slate takes advantage of being stopped at a stop sign to lean over and swipe a quick kiss onto my cheek. "Aw, Megsters, you're melting my heart. It's easier for you to love me because I'm not part of your family. If you could just take a step back and see Cam from the outside, he might not bug you so much."

"Hmm ... we'll see." Slate pulls over in front of a house where Cam stands waving to us. "I'm not sure if my legs are long enough to take a step that big."

***

With the contents of the car emptied into the garage, Cam rides back with us. We're halfway across the lawn heading toward the yoga ball rolling merrily within a small circle formed by a longboard, a set of cross-country skis, and one final garbage bag of miscellaneous stuff, when Cam's phone rings.

"Oh, hey Dad – what's up?"

"Yeah, Meg just got here. She's fine."

I nod. I'm fine. That's true.

Cam turns to me, "Hi, Meg!"

I give a half wave back and think it's lucky my dad can't see me hefting Cam's longboard under my arm. "Hi!"

"Oh, really? Yeah, delayed, I understand. OK."

Cam's quiet for a second, then says, "About that, Dad. There's this problem ..."

I note Cam's still telling the truth. There is, indeed, a problem.

"No, nothing we can't handle. Of course not. Just a small change in plans. You see, the sewers backed up ..."

Whoa. Now the lies begin.

"... yeah, you wouldn't believe the ... *shit!*" Cam's eyes have gone wide and he's flapping his arms, while saying, "No, I didn't mean shit, or, well, yeah, I guess there is ..." He mouths something at me.

"What?" I ask.

He's jutting his chin down the sidewalk, while saying, "... landlord says we need to get out of here ..." Back to the semi-truth. Now he's doing a weird kind of dance, grabbing at the garbage bag, which splits.

It's Slate who clues in. "Lauren?" she asks.

"Bingo!" Cam yells, then says, "Yeah, bingo, Dad. It means no problem. Don't worry. Meg and I will take care of everything."

Meanwhile Slate's grabbed my arm and whirls me to face a figure striding along the sidewalk. "I think that's Lauren!" she hisses.

"Oh!" I say. "Oh, *shit* ..."

I thrust the longboard at Slate. "Here, take this to the car. I'll kick the yoga ball to you!"

I kneel by my brother's side who is completely uselessly trying to wrestle his things into the bag while attempting to sound breezy and casual to my dad. "Uh-huh. Looking forward to it, too ... yep ... I will ... OK, bye."

He ends the call just as I get the last item in the bag and bends over as I wrestle with the ties. "No time!" he says. "I don't want to see her. You hold that end, and I'll hold this end. We can tie it in the car."

Cam dives into the backseat and I shove the bag in after him. I'm jumping into the passenger seat when the girl, now just a few houses away, starts running, yelling, "Hey!"

"Go!" Cam yells at Slate.

"What about the skis?" I ask.

"Leave them!" It's a moot point, anyway. Slate's already driving away. Cam and I both stare back at the girl on the sidewalk with her fists in the air.

"Man, I don't even know her and I think she looks pissed," I say.

"Yup," Cam says. "Leaving the skis will be the icing on the cake. They were a gift from her."

Chapter Eight

I sit in the terminal building and watch Slate's taillights turn left to head toward the highway and the rest of her trip.

It's warm in the waiting lounge, but outside the temperature is falling along with the October dusk.

This was not the plan.

Right about now I was supposed to be using the twenty-dollar bills my dad slipped me to pay for subs, or pizza, or burgers, or whatever my brother and I decided to have for dinner. Followed by a movie, in the theatre, or at Cam's house, and maybe a quick trip to the grocery store to stock up on food for tomorrow's breakfast.

Clearly none of that will be happening now.

Slate's lights have mingled in with all the other taillights on the road, and I turn back to face my brother.

"So." I raise one eyebrow.

"So?" He lifts his own eyebrow in return. It was only recently that I learned not everybody can do this – raise only one eyebrow – but Cam and I can both manage it. We're also both left-handed. It's the small things like this that make me believe we're actually brother and sister despite being completely different in every other way I can think of.

"So, what was that phone call with Dad?" I ask.

"Oh, that. Yeah, so apparently Mom's flight's been pushed back an hour, which means she'll probably miss the first train she was going to catch, and Dad just had a big showing scheduled for tomorrow ..."

"On Thanksgiving Sunday?"

"I mean, are you surprised?"

I shrug. "I'd have to be pretty stupid to be surprised. I just ... he never says no."

"I don't know if you've noticed, but neither of our parents really knows the meaning of the word chill. Or relax. Or any other synonym. No wonder you're the way you are."

I sit bolt upright. "Excuse me? What way am I?"

"Come on Meg – look at you now – all ramrod spine and furrowed forehead." He scrunches his own forehead to demonstrate. "You're not exactly an easy-going teenager."

"I'm completely easy-going!"

"When you say it in that tone of voice, I can see how wrong I was."

I curl my hands under my seat and clench my fists. I know how this goes. When I'm the one being accused of being uptight, there's no way to successfully fight it because my brother will turn everything I say back against me as an example of just how high-strung I really am, while vindicating whatever bad act he's accused of.

He wasn't wrong for killing the spider plant I brought home from science class in grade six and kept alive ever since – I was a killjoy for not joining in with his indoor frisbee game. It wasn't his fault we both got in trouble for eating all the chocolates out of our advent calendars by December eleventh – it was my fault for admitting we'd done it.

As much as it kills me to bite my tongue, long experience tells me there's no benefit in continuing to protest. I, personally, think it's very Zen of me to just let the topic go.

Of course Cam would probably see it as a further sign of my repression.

Just don't care, I tell myself. *Let it go. You know you're right.*

And, thankfully, as though he never detoured from the topic of my parents' travel plans, Cam loops right back to them. "Anyway, they'll be getting here late, and neither of them will have time to pick up groceries for Thanksgiving dinner ..."

"So, pizza?" I ask it with hope. I've never been a fan of turkey. My goal is to one day have pizza for Christmas dinner – plain cheese because then you can taste the sauce and there's lots of stringy, chewy mozzarella.

"I don't know, exactly."

"What do you mean?"

He shrugs. "I said we'd take care of it."

"You what?"

"I couldn't really get into details with him, what with my crazy ex-girlfriend advancing toward me, and me really needing Dad not to find out what was going on, so I just said 'we'll take care of it.' Or something like that ..."

"Was that the 'bingo' thing"? When you told him 'bingo' means 'no problem?'"

"Possibly."

"You total idiot. Cooking a turkey dinner is a problem. It would be hard enough at home, but how are we supposed to do it in the cottage, with no groceries, and no internet ..."

"We don't have to really cook a turkey."

"What do you mean? You heard Dad before. He said Mom has her heart set on a Thanksgiving dinner. And you told him we'd take care of it."

"I mean, yeah, take care of it. Like be around. Be a family. Be thankful together."

I shake my head. "I think you're wrong."

He grins. "Well then we have something in common." He punches my shoulder. "We'll figure it out."

"We'll figure it out? Are you serious?" My stomach rumbles in a perfectly timed growl. "Have you even 'figured out' what we're eating tonight? Because I'm starving."

"Well, it seems like this would be a good opportunity for you to have your pizza. We can grab a large combo at the island pizzeria."

"I don't like pepperoni."

"Fine. A large vegetarian. Whatever. You know you love their pizza."

He's right. The island pizzeria is way better – and cheaper – than anything we would have picked up on the mainland.

Still ... "How are we going to get to the cottage? Didn't Dad wonder about that?"

I've got him there. The cottage is ten kilometres from the ferry dock. I'm all for 10K – when I'm wearing running clothes, in the daylight. The dark has fallen swiftly and deeply, the wind scuttles dry leaves across the lit area at the front of the ferry building, and both Cam and I have duffel bags at our feet.

We're not going to be running any 10K to the cottage.

He shrugs. "I told Dad I'd figure it out."

"You'll figure that out too? You have a whole lot of figuring in your future."

"It's fine," he says. "I can handle it. Everything will work out."

I wrinkle my nose, squint at him through half-closed eyes. I can almost hear Slate's voice in my head. *'He's right, you know. Everything does work out for Cam. Let this be on him.'*

Cam drops onto the bench next to me and sweeps his arm toward the lake which I know is out there even though dark has fallen so thickly I can't see it. "This is for the best, Sis. Imagine waking up on the island tomorrow morning. The sky will be that crazy-ass October blue, and the apple trees will be covered, and you won't be able to think over the honking of the ducks and geese."

This is how Cam charms his way through life. Because now my head is full of the autumn island beauty and I'm almost ready to concede this fresh, new Plan B is much, much better than Plan A.

Almost.

There's still a churn in my gut, and knots in my shoulders, and a low-level pain tugging at my temples but, under Cam's fancy words and evocative descriptions is a deep truth – it's not like we have anywhere else to sleep tonight.

The lights of the ferry are sweeping around the corner into the pier, lighting up the entire docking area outside. The big boat's ready to snug up against the loading dock.

"If we're on the hook for dinner tomorrow, shouldn't we get some groceries before we go to the island?"

"No time, Sis! Boat's here and you're hungry." My brother reaches for my bag, throws it over his shoulder, and strides toward the terminal doors. "We'll worry about that tomorrow. We'll figure it out!"

Of course we will. We'll figure everything out.

I scamper after him and grab the door right before it closes in my face.

Chapter Nine

I settle onto one of the molded plastic benches in the ferry passenger lounge. My brother's browsing the bulletin boards. Drop-in yoga at the community centre. Bring your own mat, Rehearsals start after Thanksgiving for the nativity play at the Catholic school, Edna and Charlie are celebrating 65 years of marriage – all welcome to a reception at the church hall.

My phone vibrates and my heart flutters with it. Let it be Heather saying I talked to my friend. She's happy for you to try Major. Come on by anytime. Please let it be Heather.

It's not Heather.

It's my mother. How did things go with Royal?

I'm not ready to discuss this. I need to be prepared. Armed. I need to know where things stand with Major before I can talk about this.

I have to answer her.

No you don't.

I don't know if the voice in my head is Slate's or Cam's. I just know its message is so, so different from my instincts.

There's more than one way to lie. It's what I've been taught – what I believe. Omission is lying, too.

Lying is bad.

Lying is sometimes necessary.

This time I'm sure. That's what my brother would say.

I start half-a-dozen different replies in my head. Fine. Great – details later. Terrible – details later. Let's talk about it when I see you tomorrow. They're all lame. Wrong. Don't satisfy me. Won't satisfy her.

Then the phone throws up a warning banner. Low battery, It tells me. Please charge soon. Well that makes things simple.

I hold the power button until the phone shivers in my hand and the screen goes dark.

It feels wrong and right. It fills me with relief.

My dad will tell my mom Cam and I have headed to the island, if he hasn't told her already. She knows my cell coverage is spotty over there. She won't expect an answer.

I'm rationalizing. Which is another form of lying.

Which is sometimes necessary.

There! I feel like telling Cam. *I can let things go. See?*

"Hey Cam?"

He spins on his heel. "Yeah?"

"I ..." *Forget it.* "Shove over. I want to read the bulletin board, too."

Chapter Ten

The pizza is delicious. Hot and cheesy with just the right amount of sauce. It's so good that, for a few minutes, I do what Slate would do and just enjoy each mouthful without thinking about the long stretch of night between us and the cottage.

The cold, dark cottage.

When the guy who's been serving us says, "All good to go, then?" I reach for my wallet while Cam stands up. "You betcha. Come on, Meg." He holds his arms wide as though to show me the way, which seems silly considering the counter and cash register are steps away, right in front of us, where they've always been.

As I head in that direction he says, "Nah, forget about it. I already paid Ty for the pizza and the lift."

"The lift?"

Before Cam can answer, our server returns from the kitchen. He's left his apron back there and is wearing a thick camouflage coat and jingling keys. "The chariot awaits," he says.

Trust my brother to take pizza delivery to a whole new level.

***

There's a draft blowing up the inside of my jeans. I bend forward to check it out, and am immediately sorry I did. There's a hole in the floor of the car. As I watch, the edge of the yellow centre line weaves into view.

I pull the floor mat over the hole and try not to think about it. We only have about eight kilometres left to travel. Surely the bottom won't drop out of the car before we get there.

Other than the questionable structural integrity of the car, and the incredible road and engine noise, which completely cuts me off from Cam and Ty's conversation in the front seat, it's actually kind of cozy back here – now that the hole is covered.

The darkness is sporadically broken by the warm wash of front porch lights, and of über-powerful yard lights mounted high on utility poles.

Those lights illuminate lawns, driveways, and barn yards – some neat, others run-down. Sometimes they show a barking dog running toward the car. Occasionally I see cows lining fences close to their barns.

No people, though, although I do glimpse the odd rectangular glow through living room windows. The hockey game, no doubt.

We turn off the highway and now there's no light other than Ty's car's twin beams stretching ahead along the dirt road. I lean forward to watch between the front seats as they wash over the scattered gravel, and barely touch the swaying grasses on either side.

Ahead, just at the very limit of the headlights' reach, is a flutter of movement. It's faint and fast, and I couldn't swear to having seen it, but it gives me the feeling of things out there, moving and living. It could be a wild turkey, or a feral cat. It could be a fox, or a coyote.

Directly in front of us it looks like the road ends in a thicket of vegetation. Smack in the middle of it is a checkerboard sign, with its impact diminished by the tangle of vines strangling it.

Of course we know – and it seems Ty knows – that the road takes a sharp jink left, and it's right after he's negotiated this acute turn that Cam says, "Thanks, man. Right here is great."

What?

"You sure?" Ty asks.

No ... I think, staring down the driveway which looks like a yawning black tunnel which, in the absence of vegetation, the night has poured its darkness into.

"Oh, yeah. We don't want to put you any further out of your way. It's a quick hike down the driveway from here."

And so, we're out, standing on the side of the road, and Ty's lopsided taillights (one's broken) are receding down the road and It. Is. Dark. Out. Here.

Cam rubs his hands together. "Perfect! Love that moon. Let's go!"

It's true there is a *bit* of a moon. I rack my brains for the science project I did on the phases, and figure it's probably in its first quarter phase.

It beams a cool, pale wash over the fields. It's enough to be getting on with.

We get on with it.

Cam's right that the walk's not that long, but it's long enough to let Major swim back into my head. I hope he's outside, under this very moon, right now. I hope he and Millie are keeping each other company. I hope his belly is full, and his thickening coat is keeping him warm against the temperatures which have dipped into the single digits, made cooler by the persistent fall breeze.

The thought makes me shiver, and Cam asks, "You cold?"

Well, I'm not warm.

Then I notice he's holding his trendy tuque out to me.

Oh. It's not that clicky thing from when I met Major, but my heart does soften.

"It's OK," I tell him. "I'll be fine – I don't want to stretch your tuque all out of shape." I resist the urge to add, *It would look stupid on somebody as uptight as me.*

"I don't mind," Cam says. "I just want you to be warm. Let me know if you want it after all." When he's nice like this it trips a guilt switch. I should be nicer to my brother. I should ask him what happened to make Lauren kick him out. I should tell him about Major. We should talk.

I'm opening my mouth to make a start – to say, *I'm sorry you got kicked out of your house ...* – when we reach the bottom of the porch stairs.

"I sure hope the door opens," Cam says.

I swallow my brother-sister relationship-building overture. "What?!?"

"Well, the battery in the keypad usually needs to be replaced once a year. It might be low."

As he says it, a gust of wind curls around my feet, whisking cold air up under my jacket and lifting my hair. I reach out and grab the tuque from him. "And, if it's low, then what?"

He shrugs. "There should be a back-up key behind one of these boards somewhere."

"Somewhere? Should be?"

"Well, come on. There's only one way to find out. Let's see if the keypad works."

The wooden stairs clomp hollowly under our feet. All of a sudden, the cold invades my bones; my core. It's like now that we're right up against the building, my body's ready to be warm, and the fact that it isn't makes the chill worse.

I shift from foot to foot. I should have used the bathroom back at the pizzeria. "Well?" I ask Cam.

"I need your phone."

"My phone? Why? I almost never have service here, anyway."

"I need to use it to light up the keypad numbers."

"Seriously, Cam? It's almost out of charge. I turned it off on the boat because it was at about seven per cent. Where's yours?"

"I think it fell into that bag of stuff I was frantically trying to pack as Lauren charged toward us – I haven't seen it since. Anyway, why don't you have yours charged?"

"Because I thought I'd charge it at your place. To-night. While we sat in a heated room and watched Netflix."

"Whatever. Hand it over. Seven per cent should be plenty."

I click the phone to life for him. "It's six per cent now. Be quick – it won't last much longer."

I hear a series of sharp beeps, then one final longer one, followed by a grinding, whining noise. "That's it, right?" I ask. "That's the sound of the bolt sliding back?"

"Halfway." Cam demonstrates by pushing on the door, which doesn't move. "It doesn't have enough juice to open it all the way."

"Try again."

He does, and there's a repeat of the bolt half-heartedly retracting.

That's it. My body's guard is completely down. It's been a long day, and I'm wiped, and not dressed for late-night October temperatures on a spit of land right next to an open river. My teeth chatter. "Wha-a-at n-n-now?"

Cam shakes his head. "Every time I try it drains the battery more. I think we need to look for the key."

Which is how I end up crawling around over very hard, very cold rocks, feeling in the dark along the beams under one set of stairs which Cam seems to remember is where the key definitely used to be. At one time. He's pretty sure.

I turn my head toward the other end of the porch where Cam is also on his hands and knees checking behind boards. "Do Betsy and Carl have a key?"

"They might, if they weren't visiting their daughter for Thanksgiving."

As soon as Cam stops talking, a sound drifts to my ears – it's a distorted haunting cry and, sure, it could be the neighbour's hunting dog from across the bay, or it could be a coyote from somewhere much closer – and I remember the flash of *something* flitting across the road in front of Ty's car, and I imagine that something bounding through these fields toward this cottage, and I bump my head on the bottom of the stairs as I back out and say, "That's it! It's not here. What are we going to do?"

My head hurts, and I taste salt, which either means that when I hit my head I bit my tongue hard enough to draw blood, or I'm crying and the tears are running into my mouth.

I reach to wipe at my face, but my fingers are too numb to feel anything, and it's too dark to distinguish tears from blood, so I just stand and shiver and feel sorry for myself.

Cam crawls out from his search area, and the moonlight is just strong enough for me to see him run his hand through his hair. "Here, give me your phone. I'm going to try the code again."

I click the power button and nothing happens. "It's totally dead now," I tell him. If I was crying before, I'm past it now.

Cam clumps back up the stairs to the door. "What are you doing?" I ask. "I thought you couldn't see."

"I'll feel out the buttons. I should be able to figure it out."

"Now *that* inspires me with confidence." As I listen to the beeps – slower and more tentative than the last time – I run scenarios through my head. Breaking a window. Survival camping. Hiking back out to the road and waking up the nearest neighbour. If only Betsy and Carl were here. Not only would their house be warm – it would be welcoming. But they're hundreds of kilometres away and I'm alone under a vast black sky with my brother, and no key, no phone ... nothing of any use.

Then ... "grr ... rrup" followed by a sucking noise as the weather-stripping releases its grip on the door.

It takes me a second to register that the cottage is open. That we can go inside. That I'm going to sleep under a roof, inside four walls, in a bed owned by our family tonight.

Then the haunting howl comes again, and I jump up from my cold seat on the step and bound inside the cottage.

Chapter Eleven

Inside the cottage is no warmer. The air has the dead, cold feeling of unused buildings left with no circulation, no ventilation, no *life*.

Cam holds up his hand. "High five, Sis."

I stare at him. Pull my coat closer around me. "High five for what, exactly?"

"We're in!"

"We're in a cold house, with cold water, and an empty fridge."

"It'll heat up by morning, and there will be warm water then, too, and even if it's not warm in here right now, at least there's no wind."

Don't say anything. Don't engage. You're tired and cold. It will only lead to a fight.

I yank my boots off and head for the stairs.

"Hey, Sis. Where you going?"

"To bed."

"No way. I can boil the kettle. We'll have a hot drink."

I take the first step.

"Sis?"

... two, three, four ...

"Come on, there's probably a packet of hot chocolate and I bet I can find some marshmallows."

I keep climbing. Until something thwacks me in the back of the head. I whirl around in time to see a pouch of hot chocolate hit the stair below me.

Cam wanted me to let loose? Well, here goes: "Would you just back off?!?" The vehemence in my voice scares me. Also, now that I've started I can't stop. "Oh my God, Cam, it's all about you, isn't it? Everything is about you. You're not ready to go to bed, so I should stay up in a cold house and have a crappy, watery hot chocolate with you. You get it in your head that we should come over here tonight, so you drag me with you – even though you're totally unprepared and we could easily still be out there with the wolves ..."

"There are no wolves ..." He shuts up when I give him my most vicious glare. "Sorry. Continue, please."

"I was supposed to be having a day with my best friend, finding a horse – we were going to have *cupcakes* – but you had to hijack that, too. Because – what even happened this time? – you ignored Lauren's birthday, or you couldn't be bothered to buy milk, or toilet paper, or *anything* for the house *ever*, or maybe you pulled the good old 'sleeping with her best friend' trick? Whatever it was, it wasn't your problem for long, was it? Because you just made it my problem, and Slate's, and it all turned out fine for you."

I should probably stop there. That's more than enough. But I'm on a roll. Turns out when I take the controls off, they're hard to put back on.

"And, of course, it's still all about you, because I have to lie to Mom and Dad or else Mom's stress levels will spike, and Dad will lose it, and after we get the lecture of a lifetime, they'll finally, finally cut you off, and as to me getting what I want ..."

My breath – what I have left of it – is clouding in the air in front of me. I bend down to pick up the hot chocolate packet and throw it back at him. "Knock yourself out – have all the hot chocolate you want – I'm going to bed!"

Chapter Twelve

Honking, squawking, quacking – I wake to a deafening range of bird sounds, punctuated occasionally by a massive flurry of wingbeats against water, after which there's quiet for a few seconds, until the wall of noise builds again.

I've been drifting toward consciousness for a while, but have been so warm, and so comfortable, I've resisted moving.

Now, though, the sun that's been slicing through the window, bathing my bed in a toasty glow, has shifted just enough to beam directly on my eyelids.

I lift a hand to my face and slowly open one eye. The first thing in my line of vision is the cuff of yesterday's shirt I didn't even bother to change out of. It's layered over with a flannel sheet, a wool blanket, a patchwork quilt, and a duvet. I might have needed all these layers last night, but right now I'm roasting.

When I flung myself into bed and pulled all these coverings over me, I didn't expect to sleep well. I lay tense with cold, with Major, and Royal, and Cam (and the things I said to him) and my parents (and the things

I'm going to have to explain to them) running through my head. I was prepared to spend the night tossing and turning and battling twisting, turning, dreams born of frustration and confusion, and instead I must have conked out and slept for – what? – at least eight hours, I'm guessing.

I can't believe I didn't think about Major.

I can't *believe* I didn't think about Major.

I'm thinking about him now, and the thought propels me upright in bed, with blankets falling away from me, to find the whole room is warm – not just the part hit by the sun – and I realize my brother must have turned the heat on last night.

Oh. My brother.

I have that feeling you get when you've trash talked somebody behind their back, only to find they were standing around the corner listening the whole time. Except, I didn't talk about my brother behind his back.

I don't really want to see him, and I do really want to get somewhere I'll be able to find a phone signal and see if Heather texted me. The combined push and pull of those motives hops me right out of bed and to my duffel bag, dumped by the foot of the bed when I stumbled upstairs last night.

By some stroke of great good luck, the spot where I chucked it is directly in the path of a slanting sunbeam.

My clothes are warm, shoes are warm – it's heavenly to pull them on my body.

By a second stroke of luck, the first thing I see after rubber-soling my way near-silently down the stairs, is my phone, plugged in on the kitchen counter. I'd completely forgotten the battery had run down. But, apparently, my brother didn't. Because it's not luck that charged my phone – it's Cam.

First the heat, now the phone. Did I call him selfish? A spear of guilt rushes through me.

Thank goodness my brother has never been known to be an early riser; I don't feel like eating humble pie this early in the morning. I don't know if he slept on the living room couch, or in the downstairs bedroom my parents normally use, but I'm not taking the time to look around and find out. I tiptoe to the door extra-carefully to avoid waking him.

My efforts to stay quiet are rewarded when I step onto the porch and face a family of deer, heads down eating wind-fallen apples under the apple tree on the lawn.

I flatten myself against the board-and-batten siding and watch their flicking tails, telescoping ears, twitching skin.

I think of what it would be like if Major was mine so that I could watch him graze whenever I wanted to.

I have to check my phone.

Something – not me, because I haven't moved yet – sends the deers' heads flinging up, delicate muzzles scenting the air. Tensed. Ready to run.

Then, even my flimsy human ears hear it. *Thump, thud, bang,* then *whack, creak* as the door flies open. "Hey, Sis! Oh, deer – cool!"

"Yeah, deer *backsides*," I mutter, as they bound away, white tails up, zig-zagging drunkenly through the autumn-dried grasses.

My Cam resentment comes flooding back.

He grins. "Guess they didn't want to run with us."

"Us?"

"Well, it looks like you're ready to run, and I'm running too, so *us*."

"I like running alone."

"You will be running alone – just with me beside you."

"Or maybe *behind* ..."

"When did my little sister grow a competitive streak?"

Now, I think as I leap all the porch steps in one bound and hit the driveway running.

It's not fair that Cam has such long legs. It's also not fair that his body mass index is ridiculously low – the guy's got no weight to carry around on those long, spindly legs of his.

I run every day, and I don't drink, and I eat healthy food – none of which I've ever known my brother to do – and I feel like he should be 100 metres behind me, *at least*, with those things taken into account.

But he's not.

He's beside me, keeping pace.

I do a mental checklist. My feet, ankles, legs, all feel good. The road's in good shape – gravel thrown to the side, leaving two worn strips perfect for straight, fast running.

I accelerate.

The thing is, perfect running conditions for me also mean perfect running conditions for Cam.

He speeds up, too. "Nice pace, Sis."

No kidding. We're flying.

"You've been training," he says.

Only every day.

Me not answering doesn't seem to phase him. "Me, too. I decided I needed to get serious, you know? I haven't had a drink since Labour Day, and I go to the gym, or run, at least five times a week."

"No." I clench my fists – digging my fingernails into my palms – I was *not* supposed to answer.

"No, what?" he asks.

The damage is done now. I might as well talk. "You said you decided to get serious, 'you know?' and I'm saying, 'No' I don't know."

"Oh, well, the new program in Montreal. I know Mom and Dad were hoping I'd just forget about it, and you probably thought I would, too, but I really want to make it. I'm working hard on my grades, and putting together a good application, and let's just say staying up all night, and being hungover in the morning wasn't improving the quality of my work."

The fact that my brother can converse in complete sentences while running this fast backs up his claims of a new, fitter, more virtuous Cam.

We're nearing my destination, now. The intersection where my phone coverage almost always kicks in, even on the brightest days when the communication waves soar high and free in the endless blue sky. If there's a text waiting from Heather, it should appear on my phone right around here.

I slow and wrestle my phone out of the stretchy holder high on my arm.

"What are you doing?" Cam asks.

I drop to a walk and hold the phone out, as though by pointing it in the right direction, I can make the message zoom in.

"Come on, Meg. What's up?"

"Keep running if you want," I tell him. "I'm checking my messages."

"If there are messages, they'll come in when you're running. You'll be able to read them back at the cottage."

"I might want to answer – ever think of that?" I *will* want to answer if there's a message from Heather.

The phone trills, then trills again.

Text number one is from Slate: Made it to my aunt's in time for dessert. Have you heard from Heather? Tell me ASAP if you do.

I wish.

Text number two is from my mom: Are you two managing? What did you have for breakfast? Please don't use the good dishes. I want them all clean for Thanksgiving dinner. We need to talk about Royal.

There is no text number three.

Shit. Clearly this fluttery feeling in the pit of my stomach is going to be with me a while longer.

"Shit, what?" Cam asks.

"Nothing," I say. "Never mind."

"Come on," he says. "Let's start running again and you can tell me who the texts were from while we go."

We find our way back up to our former pace, searching out the right rhythm for our feet, and our breathing.

"One was from Slate, and the other one was from Mom." For the tiniest of seconds I want to tell him about the third text. The non-text. The text I really wanted. It would be nice to talk about it with someone. Maybe not my brother, though.

Cam saves me by speaking up. "Let me guess – don't use the good towels?"

The laugh surprises me. It comes fast and genuine, straight from my core. "Ha! The good dishes, actually."

"Of course! Thanksgiving dinner wouldn't be perfect eaten off chipped plates."

"Although, come to think of it, I *would* stick to using the old beach towels after your shower if you want to avoid Mom's wrath."

Cam glances sideways. "Of course you would. That's how you retain 'most-favoured child' status."

I snort. "Me? So speaks the prodigal son."

"Prodigal! What do you think I've been doing at school? I have, actually, earned one degree and I'm not that far off a second one."

I know that. Of course I know that. I was at Cam's first graduation, when he walked across the stage, all capped and gowned and was handed a rolled-up parchment. Funny, though, how in my head he's the troublemaker, the loose cannon, of the family. Funny, too, that he thinks of me as the "most-favoured child."

Maybe Cam's not what he seems. Maybe I'm not what I seem to Cam.

Just because my legs and lungs are awake and functioning, doesn't mean my brain's ready for this. So, I change the subject. "Mom also wanted to know what we were having for breakfast."

Cam raises his hand. "Fear not. I know a thing or two about bare-cupboard cooking – in fact, I should write a cookbook – when we get back, you have your shower first, and I'll rustle us up a meal."

"Just don't use the good dishes."

"I won't if you don't use the good towels."

Chapter Thirteen

The water is skin-reddeningly hot. Which means not only did my brother remember the heat, and my phone, but after I told him off and flounced off to bed, he tromped down to the cold, dark basement to turn the water system on and make sure I could enjoy this heavenly, high-pressure, steam-filled shower.

I owe him a thank-you.

All in good time. Right now I have to think.

Nothing could be clearer to me than that I need Major. I've looked at so many horses, and had so many disappointments, I'm not up for another one.

At this point, if I lose Major ... well, I don't know what I'll do. After Goody I thought I'd be OK catch riding. Getting paid for it. Having all the riding and none of the expenses or the commitment.

That didn't exactly work out, so if my heart has to go through another horsebreak, I don't know what I'll do.

Quit riding? Join Model UN, or the debating club? Give my mom a heart attack and take up rugby after all?

Despite the warm water, I shudder. I don't want to do any of those things.

I want that horse.

My fingertips are shriveled and the bathroom's so fogged up I can't see across it to the mirror.

Time to get out.

True to his word, my brother has found us breakfast.

Oatmeal steams in two bowls, there's brown sugar and raisins in the middle of the table, and he's tapping the final grains of hot chocolate into a mug. I wonder if it's from the pouch I threw across the room last night.

I stand silently as he fills the mug from the kettle, and as I watch I notice it. The bulge in his cheek. And I remember this about him; how when he concentrates – it could be on an essay he's typing, or helping my dad clean the blades on the lawn-mower or, now, focusing on a small task – he pushes his tongue into his cheek and he chews on it. He used to do it when he played basketball, which led to him biting down so hard, his tongue bled.

That's my brother ... I clear my throat. "Thank you."

He looks up at me, blowing his floppy, wind-and-run-tousled hair off his forehead. "It was really nothing. Everything before you was made using the miracle of boiling water."

"No," I say. "I meant for turning on the heat, and the hot water, when all I did was yell at you."

"I charged your phone, too."

I nod. "Yes, you did. Thank you for that as well."

"For a girl who's never been phone-obsessed it seemed to be pretty important to you. Wanna tell me why?"

I walk over to my seat and sit in front of my bowl. "What I want to do is eat this miracle breakfast before it gets cold."

As I consume my oatmeal oozing with brown sugar I reveal a dark crack running under the glazing on my bowl. "Good job," I say. "You didn't use the good dishes."

Cam points at my head where I've turbaned my wet hair inside a threadbare towel adorned with dancing parrots. "You kept up your end of the bargain, too."

It's a little thing – a tiny, silly thing – but our shared inside joke at our mother's expense feels good. I'm not ready to let it go now.

We each take a few more bites in silence, and it's not a terrible silence, before Cam says, "I didn't sleep with Lauren's best friend, by the way."

"Oh." I choke on my mouthful of hot chocolate and have to struggle not to spit it out. Once I manage to swallow it, I say. "I didn't really think you did." It sounds lame even to me.

"Yeah, you did."

"OK, yeah. I did. But I believe you that you didn't."

As a peace offering I gather up our dirty dishes to take them to the sink. "So, what did happen?"

"I told her I was applying to the program in Montreal."

The sink is filling nicely with hot, soapy water. "I can see her feeling insecure about that, but she looked *fierce* stalking down that sidewalk ..."

Cam leans back in his chair, legs outstretched, clutching his coffee mug. Still in his running clothes he looks fit, and outdoorsy, and a bit wild. I could see a girl acting crazy over him. "Well, OK, so maybe, after she offered to switch schools and study there as well, and I said no, and she lost it on me, I went out and I might have spent the night elsewhere ... but definitely not with her best friend."

"Oh Cam. I thought you liked this one."

"I do. I did. I liked her fine, but there was no click."

I drop a bowl in the sink, and fluffy, white suds spray up and coat the front of me. "Oh!"

Cam laughs. "Wow. Maybe she was right. Does it sound that stupid to you, too?"

I turn to him, look him straight in the eye, and say what might be the most honest thing I've ever said to my brother. "No. Not at all. I know exactly what you mean."

Chapter Fourteen

Cam straightens in his chair, places his mug on the table and looks back at me – really looks at me. "Is that what the early morning run to check your messages was all about? Is there a guy?"

I sigh. "There's kind of a guy. But not in the way you're thinking. He has four legs." And I start to tell my brother, who moved away from home when I was still wearing jodhpurs and hair bows, and riding a stout-legged, short-necked school pony named Killick, and who – to my recollection – has never seen me ride, about how I've fallen in love with a horse our mother will hate.

"But I can't help it," I say. "When I saw him it just clicked."

"Tell me more," Cam says.

And I do.

**

"If you feel that way, we have to go."

"What?" I ask. "But ..." I say.

"Tell me this, Sis. Are you going to be able to forget this horse?"

"No." No hesitation, no doubt.

"That makes it clear as anything. If you're still going to be thinking about something in a week, in a month, in six months, you have to do something about it. That's how I know I want to study in Montreal. It's also how I know breaking up with Lauren is the right thing to do."

"She's not a six-month girl?"

"I'm forgetting about her already."

"Ouch ..." I say. "Seriously though Cam, it's nice to say we have to go, but how?"

He points to the east wall of the cottage. "That shed out there is full of bikes."

"Bikes?!?"

"Oh, sorry, I thought you were fit. I thought you were strong. I thought this was a six-month horse ..."

"He's more than a six-month horse!"

"Then it seems like you wouldn't let a little bike ride stand in your way."

"OK, but that will take forever. What about Thanksgiving dinner?"

"Well, according to you, we have to go over to the grocery store anyway, so we might as well do this while we're there."

"Sure. Yeah. I mean since we'll be on the mainland, what's an extra thirty- or forty-kilometre round trip?"

He shrugs. "Honestly, Sis, I think this is just one of those times where we've got to wing it."

"Wing it?" Just saying those two words clenches my stomach. "If we wing it, that means we could crash and burn."

"It also means we could soar and triumph."

I snort. "Soar and triumph?"

Cam grins. "Get what we want."

"Get what *I* want ... *maybe*. If this goes wrong, Cam, not only will Mom and Dad be so furious I'll probably never have *any* horse in the world, no matter what, but it could be the nail in the coffin for your Montreal move. Have you thought of that?"

"Here's the deal, Meg. Ultimately you decide if you want a horse, and I decide where I go to school. Mom and Dad can make it easier, or harder, but those are our decisions."

"Easy to say, but they can make it *really* hard. And it could take *years* for us to do those things on our own. And you know Dad will lose it if we mess this up for Mom ..."

Cam's shaking his head. "You're making more of this than you need to."

"I'm not. I told you, Mom was all, 'Don't use the good dishes,' – that shows she's expecting something big –

and Dad was all, 'Don't ruin this for your mother.' We need to produce."

"No. You've been living at home alone for too long. You don't have perspective. As long as we're here tonight, and we're sweet, and smart, and witty, and adorable – which, let's face it, is my natural state – we're golden."

I open my mouth to protest and Cam cuts me off by spreading his arms, and holding his palms up. "Bottom line, Meg, are we going for it, or not?"

He's got me there, because even though my instincts are to play it safe – even though I'll be on edge all day long, until we're safely back here, sitting at the Thanksgiving dinner table with my parents – now that my brother's raised the possibility of going to see Major, the thought of *not* doing it is completely impossible. It would also have me on edge all day. And for the rest of the weekend. And for the next week, month, six months when that horse isn't part of my life.

"Oh, fine," I say. "If it makes you happy we'll go."

"Because everything's always all about me, right?"

"That's true. You've got it."

Chapter Fifteen

This, in itself, could be enough.

Should be enough, really.

Twin strips of rubber rolling over the tire-polished asphalt. The sky big – prairie-big – except we have the added benefit of water winking all around us. As the trees lose their leaves it peeks from the vast bay on the other side of the concession road, and across the fields. When we crest the biggest (but still small) hill on the highway cutting south-north across the island we can see the stretch of river dividing us from the mainland.

We spin by fields, some shorn, others bristling with unharvested corn, while livestock graze in others.

Overhead are never-ending vees of geese. Honking, flapping, re-arranging themselves. Landing and taking off from low spots in the fields where temporary ponds make for great rest stops.

And ahead of me the tall, whippy body of my brother. Straight back, long legs, pushing his vintage bike into the wind – creating a draft which eases the way for my equally ancient ten-speed.

A dog – tongue lolling, tail wagging – runs beside us for a hundred metres. A man waves from a tractor in a field.

I'm stretching my legs, working my lungs in a place that is as beautiful as any other on earth. This is the closest I've ever felt to my brother; he's on my side, he's helping me.

But ... the churn is there, in the pit of my stomach. The tension pulls across my forehead.

All is not quite right. Not yet. I'm not with Major. He could still become somebody else's.

Every pedal stroke gets me closer, though ... that's what I keep telling myself. This one, and this one, and this one. And so I push, and pull, and stand, and sit, and pedal, and after a while we hit the dump, and that means the village is just ahead, and the ferry, and we're still nowhere near Major, but we're closer than we were back in the cottage.

A gust of wind seizes my bike and I keep pushing. *We're closer.*

***

The boat's coming. It always happens faster than I think. One minute it's a speck, just making the turn out of the protected dock on the mainland, and I think, *I have forever until it's here,* and I pick up a conversation with the person I'm waiting with, or read another chapter of my book or, today, mentally calculate how many kilometres it is to Major's barn, and how long that could possibly take on two rickety bikes, and whether there's any way at all of being back before dark.

Then I look back and it's most definitely a ferry – with a broad, flat deck flanked by passenger lounges on either side and crowned by the bridge.

This time it just takes a short, fleeting minute of distraction – of wondering how my parents are going to fit into all this. Of what they'll say when they arrive to find us not here, and of how both Cam and I will explain away, or avoid explaining, everything that's happened in the last twenty-four hours.

When I look again, the boat's looming large and coming fast, throwing a roiling bow wave up in front of it, and this is the moment – or nearly the moment – when my commitment to this horse will be tested. Just how much do I want him? Enough to get back on the bike with the saddle that's already pinching, and make that long, long trek?

I remember his warm breath on my neck and tighten my grip on the handlebars of both bikes and decide if Cam's willing to come along on this expedition, then I'd better be prepared too as well, and now my only worry is, where *is* Cam?

When we pulled up at the dock, with my lungs still sucking in extra oxygen, and my legs tingling with hard work, Cam darted off. "Just wait here with the bikes, and I'll be back."

"Wait!" I'd said. "What?" But I had two bikes leaning on me so I couldn't chase him.

"I have an idea," is all he said, and I had to settle for that.

Now I'm waiting, and the boat's nudging the dock, and the ramp's going down, and there's no Cam in sight.

This is *not* good for my stomach. Layered on top of the underlying butterflies of seeing Major, and riding Major, and maybe, fingers crossed, owning Major, is now the grinding anxiety of *Where is my brother?* and *This is just like my brother,* and *He probably* did *sleep with Lauren's best friend,* and *He's probably seducing somebody else's girlfriend right about now.*

The first cars are lumbering off the ferry.

I should just chuck Cam's bike in the river. I should just get on by myself and head up to the highway, and the barn, on my own.

Now the final cars are bumping over the ramp, and the first car on our side is preparing to load.

Except ... it's really far to go on my own. I shake my head. That's just silly. It's the same distance with or without my brother. Somehow, though it seems like an adventure when I think of doing it with him, and it seems desperate, or crazy, or ... I don't know what, but not *fun*, to do it on my own.

But, *Major*. So, I'm going to do it.

Right ...?

"Sis!" I whip my head around. *Where is he?* "Meg! Over here! Quick!"

He's in line. Oh my God, he's in line in a car.

Confusion and joy jump inside me at the same time, then I take another look at the car and a tiny bit of gloom tinges my excitement. I know that car. It has a hole in the rear floorboards. If I can *see* that, who knows what else is wrong with it?

But it's faster than a bike – or two bikes – that's for sure.

We might make it back in time to put together some kind of mish-mashed Thanksgiving dinner. We might stay on my parents' good side.

I start toward Cam, still holding both bikes. "What about these?"

One of the young guys who works on the ferry, wearing a high visibility vest with a patchy beard that makes me think he's trying to prove he's all grown-up, walks toward me, hands out. "You want me to take care of these?"

"I, uh, yes please."

He winks. "My pleasure. They'll be behind the crew trailer whenever you want to pick them up."

OK.

"OK," I say. "Thanks!" Then I run around the car, and jump into the passenger seat – but not too hard, in case something breaks under me, like the seat, or the floor – and with a wave for the ferry guy babysitting our bikes, my brother accelerates over the ramp and onto the ferry deck.

We ease into our spot, and Cam shuts off the ignition, then turns to me. "There. Sorted. You trusted me to figure things out, right?"

I bite back a half-nervous, half-shocked giggle and make an effort to nod as slowly and calmly as I can. "Oh yes. Of course. Always."

"Great! Let's go buy a horse!"

Chapter Sixteen

"That guy liked you," Cam says.

"What? Huh?" I'm digging my phone out of my pocket. I keep checking it for a text from Heather, and there keeps being none. Even though we're on our way, I'd feel so much better if she'd just send me a message saying she talked to her friend. Saying I can try Major. Making this trip feel less like a wild goose chase and more *sensible*.

"The guy who works on the ferry. He didn't take the bikes to be polite."

"That's exactly what he did. It was very polite of him."

Cam shakes his head. "I can't wait to see the day you like someone enough to give them a chance."

I think of Lauren. And Maggie before her. And, was it Cara, or Stephanie before that? I fight to keep from laughing out loud. "Ditto."

"Ha!" Cam bumps his shoulder into mine. "Touché. I guess we're just coming at it from opposite ends of the spectrum."

My phone pings, and I immediately check it, then sigh. Fun and games over.

"You look like you just opened a present on Christmas morning and it was socks," Cam says.

"Underwear, more like."

"It's not the horse lady?"

"It's Mom."

"OK, well hang on. That could be useful. Does she say what time she'll be here?"

"She says she's waiting to board a train that's supposed to leave there in half-an-hour."

"Which means – what? – three hours until she's here?" Cam asks.

I frown. "More like two-and-a-half ..." Butterflies race through me. We're not going to be back in time. There are explanations – conflict – in my future.

"I told you, Sis. Chill. Besides, the train's probably not an express. And Dad still needs to pick her up at the train station and drive her down to the ferry dock. And maybe she'll be hungry – they might stop for food ... you're forgetting the very real world of travel delays."

I snort. "You're forgetting this is our mother. She doesn't do delays."

Cam shrugs. "Well then I guess we just won't have to do delays either. How long can it take to buy a horse?"

***

I guide my brother back along roads that already seem familiar.

We pass a sign I noticed twice yesterday. **Apples for sale.** "Mmm ... apple crisp," I say.

"We'll buy some on the way back to celebrate," Cam says.

"If ..."

"Zzt!" Cam interrupts. "No 'if.' We'll buy some on the way back."

We turn onto the wide gravel road, and I try not to picture little rocks bouncing into the back of Ty's car through the hole in the floor. Then we hit the narrow dirt lane, and rattle up the rutted driveway into Heather's stableyard.

"Here?" Cam asks, and when I nod he turns off the engine.

It doesn't take long before we see signs of life. A cat wanders out of the barn, tail up, making for the car. Two horses in the nearest paddock pause in their grazing to stare at us, chew a few times, then drop their heads again.

I'm waiting for Heather to come. Yesterday we had an appointment. Today I hesitate to just get out and wander around her property. But ... delays ... we can't afford them.

"I guess we can go look for her," I say.

"You're the boss," Cam says.

We step out of the car and, like yesterday, I stick my head in the barn. Like yesterday the light shining through from the back shows the aisle swept clean, and no sign of any life. This fall weather is far too nice for horses to be in during the day.

"Should we go to the house?" Cam asks.

"No," I say. "I don't want to bug her. If she's there she'll see our car and come out eventually."

"Why don't you text her?" Cam asks.

I shrug. Why not? Hi Heather. This is Meg. From yesterday. I pause, look at Cam. "I feel really desperate."

"You are desperate. Right?"

"I ... yeah. You're right." I take a deep breath. I'm actually here, right now, back at your place. I'm hoping you've re-thought letting me try Major.

Send. Done.

I turn to my brother. "Do you want to see him?"

"What do you think?"

The thing is, because Major came and found me yesterday, I'm not actually sure where his paddock is. But he can't be that hard to find.

I lead my brother around the corner of the barn and we come face to face with Royal. Something near the horizon has caught his attention, and he's ears forward, nostrils flared, a light arch in his neck, every muscle tensed.

"Wow," my brother says. "Nice looking horse."

"Et tu?"

"Oh, is this the one Mom likes?"

"Of course it is."

Whatever Royal noticed in the distance, he's decided it's not that important. He turns to me with an easy friendliness and I can see not only is he a gorgeous horse, but he's a nice one, too. He reaches his nose to me, and lets me scratch his neck and it's clear we could build a relationship. We could get along. We could go places together. I feel a pang of guilt for dismissing him so quickly yesterday. "He's a nice horse."

"Lauren's a nice girl," my brother says.

"Oh!" I say. "Thanks."

"Anytime. I'm always here to remind you of what's important in life."

I smile.

"What's so funny?" he asks.

"Nothing." Nothing, except that I'm pretty sure my mom would say the same thing, while meaning the exact opposite. "Let's go find Major and you can tell me if I'm being crazy."

***

He's nowhere.

We count fourteen horses, total, behind five gates. None hold a bay thoroughbred who could stand to gain a couple of hundred pounds and would benefit from a grooming make-over. No small Shetland ponies either. One is empty, but the gate's closed, so that doesn't align with Pearl's modus operandi.

"Are you sure he isn't one of the ones we saw?" Cam asks.

I give him a look. "That is such a non-horse-person question. It would be like me asking why can't you just stay here and study instead of going to Montreal."

"Because the programs are totally different … Oh. Right. Got it."

I glance at my phone. No new messages. "And Heather hasn't shown up either, which is weird … wait a minute … was there a horse trailer at the house?"

"What? Why do you want to know?"

I'm not really listening to his answer. My brain is racing, trying to picture the spot where, yesterday, a horse trailer was parked, with a cat sunning itself on the running board. The cat who, this morning, came out of the barn to greet us.

Was the trailer there when we pulled in? Did we drive by it? I just don't know, and the longer I don't know the faster my pulse races, and it keeps me from being able to think straight … "Come on!" I turn away from the grazing horses surrounding us snug in their paddocks. "We have to check."

There's no trailer. Which freaks me out enough to make me go knock on Heather's door. If she's sleeping in, or having a shower, or entertaining an overnight guest, I'll be embarrassed, and apologetic, and so, so relieved.

She's not there.

"Oh my God!" I turn to my brother. "Do you see? No horse, no Heather, no trailer. She's taken him."

"Taken him where?"

"To her friend's place. The one she was boarding him for. To his new home." I look at my brother. "Not to me."

Whoosh. All the air goes out of me and takes my reason with it, leaving a huge vacuum for panic to rush in and fill.

"That's it. I've lost him. And don't tell me I'll find another horse, because I already lost one, and Major was the second one I found – and it was a total miracle I found him and that won't happen again, and I'm running out of time to find a horse, because of university coming, and it's not about another horse, it's about this horse, *that* horse ... I loved him ... and I know that sounds stupid, but I did, and ..."

"Meg."

"No, I'm serious Cam."

"Meg!"

"What? Don't tell me to lease Royal because I swear I'll kill you ..."

"Meg. Turn. Around."

I'm still saying, "Huh ...?" as I turn and see the very trailer I was just looking for being towed off the road and up the driveway past us.

"Is that the trailer you were looking for?" my brother asks.

"It is indeed."

Now if only the horse I want would appear so conveniently.

***

We walk up to meet Heather as she climbs out of the pick-up truck.

Cam's a step behind me, and I hear him whisper, "Whoa ..."

I turn around, "What?"

"You didn't say she was hot."

"Slate should be your sister ..." I mutter.

"Huh ...?"

Heather's already saying hi, and asking, "What are you doing here?"

My heart knows what it wants, my brain knows what it wants, but do you think I can get the words out? "I ... uh ..."

Cam steps forward, hand extended. "What she's been doing, is freaking out."

Heather stops, stares at my brother's hand, and when she looks back up to his face her cheeks are washed pink. Cam pushes his hand further forward, "Hi, I'm Cam. Meg's brother."

She takes his hand and her blush deepens and spreads. "Meg's brother. Hi."

Maybe it's this place. There seems to be clicking in the air.

She doesn't even look at me. Just focuses on Cam and asks, "What has Meg been freaking out about?"

"The trailer was gone." I say. "I thought you'd taken Major."

Heather's extended handshake with Cam ends, and that seems to give her space to remember me. "No. My neighbour called this morning. She had to get her daughter and her horse to a clinic and their trailer had a flat. I just dropped them off and came back."

"Then ... where is he?"

Chapter Seventeen

For the first time I feel like I have Heather's full attention.

"What do you mean?"

"I looked for him – *we* looked for him everywhere. We couldn't see him in any of the paddocks."

"He's in the southwest paddock, with Millie, the Shetland I told you about."

I shake my head. "No Major. No Millie."

Heather looks at Cam as though he can clear this up, and he shrugs. "If she says there's no Scotland pony out there, there's no pony."

"Shetland," I say.

"What?"

"Never mind ..." I'm filling with antsiness again. "Just come with me?" I ask Heather. "I'll be so, so happy if you can show me I was wrong."

She can't.

The three of us stand in front of the closed gate, staring at the cropped-down grass, and Heather says. "Oh."

"Look." It's true the gate is closed, but I point at the chain which isn't actually attached to anything. It's just hanging over the rail enough to keep the gate from swinging open.

"Looks like Pearl must have been here after all," Heather says.

"So, what does that mean?"

She shrugs. "It's normally not a big deal. She usually takes Millie back to their house and eventually one of the kids notices, and brings her back, and it's all fine. But, yeah, like you saw yesterday, she's let Major out a couple of times and he's just wandered around here, grazing on the lawn, and raiding the apple tree."

I turn, slowly, in a big circle taking in the unraided apple tree and the unshorn lawn. We can all see he's not here.

My brain floods with worry. Where could he be? I think of the massive unfenced expanse of Blister Park. *Anywhere* is where he could be.

What next? I have no idea. We didn't really have time to come here anyway, there's no way we have time to mount a search and rescue for a wayward horse.

The sensible thing would be to walk away. To say 'At least we tried.' To leave Heather to solve this problem and to move onto solving ours ... I don't even want to think about how many hours we have left and how many hours it takes to cook a turkey.

My brother lays his hand on my shoulder and I turn to him and wait for his cooler head – unclouded by equine love-at-first-sight – to prevail. Brace myself for him to say, 'I'm really sorry, Sis, but we have to go.'

"Yes?" I ask.

He looks at his watch and I wince. *Tick-tock.* "I know ..." I start.

"Which way do you want to go?" he asks.

"Pardon me?"

"You pick the direction and I'll go the other way. We'll decide on a time to meet back here."

"You ... really?"

"Of course," he says. "What else would we do? We came all the way out here. We're not just walking away."

"I ... oh ... I ..." Cam's reassurance has settled my mind enough to let me form an idea. "I think I know where to go."

"OK. You tell me where you're going and I – and maybe Heather?" He looks at her, eyebrows lifted, "Can look other places."

Heather blushes again. "Sure, yes. We can go together."

"Great!" Cam smiles at her. "I wouldn't know what to do with a horse if I found him." He winks at me. "Don't worry. We'll sort this out."

***

I'm on the dirt road, walking toward Pearl's house. "You can't miss it," Heather said. "It's the first driveway in that direction." Then she and my brother headed the other way.

I scan the woods for signs of a tall skinny horse or a roly-poly Shetland pony. Nothing.

I scour the road and, sure enough, there are hoofprints, but that means very little to me. They could be an hour old, they could be days old.

Up ahead is a mailbox. Good, I'm almost there. *Please let him be here.* I cross the fingers of both hands, then I'm afraid to uncross them again. If I do, he won't be here. Or, worse, if I do, I'll find out he was here, but he's gone again. Or he'll be hurt. Or ... I make a deal with myself. If I see Major, uninjured, I'm allowed to uncross my fingers so I can lead him home.

OK. *Breathe. Look.*

Up the driveway, narrow and hemmed in with trees. A dog runs out – at least part border collie – head low, tail sweeping, nudging my leg then falling into step beside me. I scratch his ears as best I can with my contorted hands. "You're no guard dog, are you?" I lift my voice, make it breathless and excited. "Where are the horses?"

He pricks his ears and tilts his head.

"Horses?" I repeat.

He gives a little whine and trots ahead of me.

I follow him into a clearing nestling a dormered house surrounded by a wrap-around porch low to the ground. On it a woman sits in a chair and next to her is a shaggy pony, eyes half-closed, head resting just above her lap.

Steps away, head down to the lawn is the object of my dreams, hopes, and wishes for the last not-quite twenty-four hours. The creature I've pinned my happiness to. The one I've been sure I can't do without.

"Major?" I say, and he lifts his head and takes a step forward, then another, until he's close enough to blow warm breath into my outstretched hands – fingers uncrossed – then drop his head back to the nice green grass.

His coat is just as dull and choppy as I remember, his body is too thin for his height, his neck – now that I really look at it – has a caved-in, no-muscle-at-all look, and I'm not in the least disappointed and I definitely haven't changed my mind. I twine my fingers through his uneven mane, and every bit of stress and worry leaves me.

"That's nice," says the woman on the porch.

I look at her. "Yes. It is. Are you Pearl?"

"Yes I am dear. And this is Millie."

"Millie's lovely," I say.

"Yes dear. She is – to me, anyway."

"Well, that's all that matters."

The door opens and another woman – younger – steps out on the porch. A familiar smell drifts out with her – the scent of roasting turkey – *oh, yeah ...*

"Hello," she says.

"Hi," I say. "I've come from Heather's. We were looking for Major here, and we thought he might have come over with Millie and Pearl."

The woman claps her hand to her chest. "I am so sorry. Grandma does bring Millie over quite often, but she's never brought this horse – is he OK?"

I laugh. "It's OK. I'm just happy to have found him. He seems absolutely fine – I think he likes your lawn."

"Is he yours?"

I suck in a deep breath, cross my fingers again before exhaling. "I hope he will be."

Pearl speaks up. "He should be, dear. I can see the love. It's very clear."

The younger woman rests her hand on Pearl's shoulder. "My grandmother has always had a way with horses – she used to breed and train Standardbreds for the track – if she says you and that horse have a connection, she's right."

"Thank you," I say. Part of me wants to stay here indefinitely, with my favourite horse in the world grazing at my feet, and this interesting woman telling me things

I want to hear, but the turkey smell is powerful in my nostrils. "Unfortunately, I do need to get going. Do you mind if I take Major back now?"

"Of course not, dear. He should go with you." I like Pearl more and more by the minute.

"I'm sorry for any inconvenience," the granddaughter says. "Is there anything I can do for you?"

I hesitate. "There is one thing."

"Yes?"

"Could you please tell me how long it takes to cook a turkey?"

Chapter Eighteen

I walk Major back along the narrow driveway using the halter and lead I brought with me.

I like the way he moves next to me; long colt-like legs swinging along. Head held at the level of mine, so I can see where his ears swivel, so we could have a conversation if we needed to.

I'm happy to be quiet for a while. After all, there's not much to say.

Not to him.

I fell for him, I was afraid I lost him, I found him again, and being with him is as great as I thought it would be.

I reach out and rub the crest of his neck. "It's not you I have to talk to, is it?"

Heather. She's the one I have to convince.

And, oh yeah, eventually Craig, and my parents.

My parents ... it's going to be easier to get them on my side if they're filled with turkey, and wine, and the joy of a family Thanksgiving.

Based on Pearl's granddaughter's Coles Notes of turkey-cooking, Cam and I don't have any time to spare.

At the end of the driveway I stop, and Major stops too. "Seems like a good time for multi-tasking – what do you think?"

I need to give him a trial ride and I need to get back to Heather's as quickly as possible.

There's a big tree stump just behind the mailbox. Major follows me to it willingly and when I ask him to halt, stands still beside it.

"Do you mind if I get up?" I ask. I'm already on the stump, running my hands over Major's back, and sides, adding weight to see if that sends him skittering away.

He turns and looks at me, but doesn't move.

On the one hand, this is a dumb idea. He's a former racehorse who, for all I know, might never have been ridden off the track at all. He's young, he's in an unfamiliar setting, and as much as I fell in love with him at first sight, I know very little about him.

On the other hand, if he's flighty, and / or nervous, and / or doesn't want me on him, in theory he'll just sidestep away from me when I try to get on and that will be a somewhat awkward, and not-very-elegant end to that idea.

Turns out, even if I don't fall this isn't going to be elegant. The stump's not quite high enough to provide easy access to mounting his sharp-withered back, so I have to go in shuffling, tiring, clumsy stages.

First, I fling myself as far across his narrow back as I can. Then I struggle to get my right leg all the way over his body without giving him a hearty kick in the rump. Finally I scooch my way into the spot where my seat fits nicely into the dip of his back, and my legs curve around his barrel.

He's a prince through all this – waiting patiently while I find my balance – not even doing so much as twitching his skin.

And, when I'm finally in the right spot, it's perfect. I don't feel like an oversized giant the way I do when I drill Peanut and the other schooling ponies. I don't feel like I'm going to walk bow-legged for a day like I do every time I ride the broad-barreled Charisma.

Even the hogsback-like ridge of his withers – which, I'll admit, I eyed with apprehension – doesn't cause a problem. I give it some respect; keep my weight back, and everything's fine.

In lieu of clucking, or squeezing, or nudging, I just say, "OK. Walk on," and he does, and we're moving together and, "Oh, you are just the nicest boy ever!"

I love the view between his forward-pricked ears of the country road tinged with that sepia-toned quality sunlight only carries at this time of year. I love the steady, easy sound of his hooves scattering gravel into the roadside tangle of grasses and wildflowers past their summer prime. I love the warmth of his body beneath me, and the heat of the sun on my back. I love the mingling of the sharp scents of autumn – cool pockets of air not yet reached by the sun, wood smoke from somebody's bonfire, and the smell of Pearl's family's turkey trapped in my nostrils – combined with the warm horsey scent rising from Major. And I love the feel of moving with this horse – swaying to his walk and, yes, even jouncing like a complete novice when we trot. I feel unbalanced, I feel rattled, I feel like a bouncing mess of unsteady hands and swinging legs, but he's tolerant. He keeps trotting. Maybe I don't look as bad as I feel. Maybe it doesn't matter.

I try to post, and that makes things better. I regain my sense of rhythm, and – with no bridle to rely on – we swing into Heather's driveway based solely on the turn of my head, and the pressure of my leg and the lead rope draped against Major's neck, and my rather silly instruction to, "Turn here, boy."

Heather and my brother are straight ahead of us, by the barn, sitting on the lowered tailgate of her pick-up truck, now unhitched from the trailer.

Fifty metres from them Major slows to a walk, and pulls up completely right in front of them. Heather reaches out to stroke his muzzle. "You found him."

"You don't sound surprised."

She shields her eyes from the now-very-strong sun. "Your brother said you'd find him."

I nudge Cam's shoulder with the toe of my paddock boot. "Cam tends to believe things will work out."

I slide off Major's back, with my butt and legs leaving behind a shiny, flat zone in the middle of the cold-weather fur of the rest of his coat. It will fluff up soon, but for now, I rest my hand there – maintain our connection.

My mind is whirling with conflicting priorities. We have to go, to make sure we keep our parents happy, to make sure my parents will let me have Major ... but, there's no point in that if Heather isn't going to let me have Major, so I have to convince her, which is going to take time ...

First things, first, I guess. I hand the lead to Heather. "I met Pearl. She seems nice. But, maybe ..."

"Maybe not turn this guy out with Millie anymore?"

"Not if you don't want him to go missing again."

"I definitely don't. He's only my responsibility for a little while longer and his new owner would be pretty mad if I lost him."

Ooh. Stab to the heart. Kick to the gut. New owner. "About that ..." I take a deep breath, try to find Cam's eyes for reassurance, but Major's neck is in the way. "Is there any chance you think you could check with your friend? See if she'd consider selling him to me, instead? I've ridden him now, you see ..."

"And you still want him? Even after barebacking behind those ridiculous withers?"

"They're not that bad."

Heather laughs. "You're in deep, aren't you?"

I don't even know what to say anymore. Heather laughing is not helpful. And where is Cam? Why is my "let's-go-get-you-a-horse brother" suddenly so quiet? I could use his back-up right about now.

"Listen," Heather says. "I don't need to call her."

I'm sorry I ever dismounted. If I was still on Major's back I could just gallop away with him and sent Heather an eTransfer later. It's not stealing if you pay, right?

Heather's still talking. "... main thing is for him to have a good home."

"Pardon me?"

"She said she never had her heart set on this particular horse – and, realistically, a Heinz 57 about two hands shorter than this guy would make a much better trail horse – but she saw a post that this guy was going to auction if someone didn't step in, so she did."

"So ... that means ..."

"So, that means, if you want him, she'll sell him to you for the cost of what she's already spent on him, and she'll rescue another horse."

"What?" There's a squeal in my voice that prompts Major to lift his head out of the way, revealing my wide-smiling brother. "You!" I yell, and fling myself against him.

The hug is strong. It lasts a long time. It's the first one I can remember for years.

While I'm hugging Cam, Heather says, "Your brother already eTransferred me a deposit."

"Wow," I say. "Thank you," I say. "I'll pay you back."

"We'll talk about it in the car," he says.

"Oh yeah!" I straighten. "We'd better get going because I talked to Pearl's granddaughter about turkey cooking times and, short story, we are screwed."

"Oh well, I guess you'll get your pizza Thanksgiving wish after all."

"Nope! Not to worry. We'll figure it out." I'm counting on my brother's own line keeping him quiet and I'm right.

He just smiles and says, "OK, whatever. Off we go."

Chapter Nineteen

Driving away this time should be easier, but a piece of my heart, and a chunk of my mind are left behind with Major who, last I saw, was very happily occupied with a haynet and some solo turn-out time in the carefully gated sand ring.

"What happened?" I ask Cam. "How did you make that happen?"

He shrugs. "I mean, nothing crazy. While we were crawling along in the pick-up truck at fifteen kilometres an hour, I just explained things to her. It's not like she's unreasonable."

"When we got back, I asked what anybody had to lose by her just calling her friend and asking, so she did. And the rest is history."

"What about the money? How much do I owe you? Do you even have it?"

As he indicates to turn onto the highway he flashes me a trademark Cam smile. "Fortunately, I hadn't quite gotten around to paying my October rent yet – and now it looks like I'm not going to need to – so I just transferred over half of that. Money well spent."

***

"OK, here's the plan ..." With Major safe and secured, the Thanksgiving dinner worry can once again move to the front of my brain. After all, I still need to convince my parents Major's the horse for me, and that we need to send a trailer to bring him home to Craig's. "... Pearl's granddaughter said we should buy turkey breasts – they should sell them in the meat section – because they cook a lot faster than a whole turkey and, besides, we don't need a whole turkey for four people."

"I still don't think we need a whole turkey at all. Just buy turkey slices. And some of that really cheap but insanely delicious white bread. And a big jar of mayo ... mmm ... I'm drooling just thinking about it."

I fish around and find a pen and an old receipt in my bag. "This is me ignoring you while I make a list of real, actual, delicious Thanksgiving food." I look at my watch. "If you drop me off by the grocery store I'll have time to run in and grab the food while you get the car in line and we should be on the next ferry."

Cam sighs. "Hey, if you want to kill yourself it'll be your funeral. Whatever you do, make sure you definitely get the white bread – and the mayo – if we're going to have turkey tonight, I definitely want turkey sandwiches tomorrow."

***

I close Ty's car door and cross the street while my brother accelerates away.

Note to self – if they sell gas station gift cards in the grocery store, I should buy one for Ty. Without him – his car, anyway – I wouldn't have Major.

I'm patting my pocket to make sure it holds the list I just made. I'm rummaging in my bag to make sure it holds my wallet containing my dad's still-unspent twenty-dollar bills.

I walk up to the sliding glass doors of the grocery store and nearly run into them.

Why are they not opening?

Wait a minute ... it's awfully dark in there.

I take a step forward and spread my palm on the immobile glass.

There's nobody in there.

Take a step back and note the completely full ranks of shopping carts and the really-quite-empty parking lot.

That's when my eyes finally settle on the sign listing the opening hours – such an everyday thing I didn't notice it before – except, of course, this week things are different. This week contains a fairly major holiday.

Which is today.

The store closed early. I look at my watch; forty-seven minutes ago, to be precise.

Crap. Damn. Hell.

I so do *not* have this figured out.

***

As I wait for the light to change I peer across the street, past the terminal building, and the special parking area for oversized trucks and trailers, and scan the cars in line. My eyes light on the familiar car and all I can think about is getting there as quickly as possible and sinking into the passenger seat to say, "Holy shit, Cam – what are we going to do?"

I hurry across the street, stride past the terminal building – past a tractor-trailer, and an open-sided livestock truck rustling with cows, and somebody's jeep with an ATV lashed to a trailer behind it – then I look for the shortest route from here to the car and point my feet that way.

Except ... *Oh. My. God.* I freeze. My heart hammers. I can barely breathe.

It's the wrong car.

I finally get a strong enough grip on my brain and body to shrink back, into the shadow of the tractor-trailer.

The car I saw, and recognized, and naturally headed toward is, indeed, one I'm very familiar with. It's our family car. The one my dad would have driven from our house this morning. The one he would have used to pick my mother up. And now they're here. I can't believe they're already here.

So, where's Cam?

I look up and down the rows of cars and, now that I'm actively looking for it, find Ty's.

It's parked about halfway along the second row which is no-problem-you're-definitely-getting-on-the-ferry territory. My parents, on the other hand, are in the zone where you usually get on the boat, but depending on other factors will sometimes get left behind.

My hand brushes the grill of the tractor-trailer. Factors like how many oversized vehicles get loaded before your car.

Our only hope is for my parents to get left behind.

The car line tells a story – Cam must have pulled into line right before one of those occasional flurries of cars that sometimes happens. It's like everybody decides to head for the ferry at the same time and the line grows by a dozen cars in just a few minutes. My parents must have just gotten here. There's only one car behind them.

The oversized line, not so much. Without actually seeing these vehicles arrive – which, of course, I didn't – I have no concept of which ones arrived when. The ferry workers on the dock will have been paying attention so they can load the ones that were here before the ferry was full, and make the others wait for the next boat.

Even as I'm running all this through my head, a small RV pulls into an empty space close to the terminal building. If only all these vehicles – including the new RV – are put on the ferry, I'm almost positive my parents won't make it.

That would give Cam and me an hour's head start.

Which, granted, isn't much, but it would at least let us raid the general store – see what food they have – if the general store's even open ... *worry about that later.*

We'll figure it out.

"Hey! Going back to pick up your bikes?" I turn to see the ferry worker from this morning standing in front of me, smiling.

My mind races. *That guy liked you.* If it's even a little bit true, it could be very good for me.

I am *so* not good at this. I'll always tell people – mostly Slate – the reason I've never had a boyfriend is that I have yet to meet a guy better-looking than a horse, but that's only part of the truth. I've just never been inspired enough by any guy I've met to make an effort, to flirt, to put myself out there.

Right now, though, I'm feeling a little more inspired.

I blink, open my eyes wide and look up at him. "Gosh, yes, thanks so much for helping with that. My brother ..."

"Oh, that was your brother? I thought he was, maybe, your boyfriend."

I widen my eyes just a little bit more. "No. Not at all. If I had a boyfriend that annoying I wouldn't keep him around for long."

"Yeah? Your brother get on your nerves?"

"Often," I say. "In fact ..."

"In fact, what?"

I shake my head. "No. Forget it. You don't want to listen to my problems. You've already helped me today."

"Tell me. I'll help again if I can."

"We-e-ell. OK. It's like this. My brother and I need to get back to the island before my parents, but he took so long while we were over here I've just noticed my parents' car is in line behind us – that one; the silver SUV. We were counting on having an hour before they made it over. Now we're kind of screwed."

"Have a party at your place last night? Need to clean it up?"

"Something like that."

"Yeah, I know what that's like." He scratches his head, looks over at my parents' car, then at the tractor-trailer. "I'd say they're out of luck, wouldn't you?"

"I ... yeah ... I mean I wasn't sure, but if you say so."

He gives two quick nods. "I say so. All these vehicles here are going on the next boat. Your parents' car isn't going to fit."

"Wow. OK. Thanks for clearing that up. I don't know what I would have done without you today."

"My pleasure," he says. "Just make sure you guys invite me the next time you have a party." He points to the harbour where the ferry's sweeping in. "You'd better get on over to your brother in that old car of Ty's."

"Yeah, thanks. You're right."

"Here." He shrugs off the bright yellow jacket he's wearing over a hoodie and his high visibility vest. "Maybe you should wear this on your way back – with the hood up – just so nobody recognizes you walking across the parking lot."

"But, don't you need it?"

"Just hand it to one of the guys on the boat – they'll get it back to me."

I scamper across the open asphalt, head down, turtled under the gaping hood of the four-sizes-too-big jacket. I yank the passenger door open and drop in and Cam jumps. "Whoa! I didn't recognize you at first."

"Just as well."

"What on earth are you doing in that jacket, and why don't you have any groceries with you?"

"It's a long story. I'll tell you on the boat."

Chapter Twenty

I push the hood down, bring Cam up to speed and ask, "What are we going to do?"

"We're going to do what I should have insisted we do all along. We're going to go into the pizzeria, and order a couple of pizzas – maybe they'll even have one with turkey on it in celebration of the holiday – and you can have a Diet Coke, and I'll have a beer, because I don't have to drive anymore, and we'll meet Mom and Dad coming off the next ferry and we'll all drive back to the cottage with our pizzas and give thanks for being together as a family."

I bite my lip, wrinkle my nose. My brain races and so does the nervous energy cartwheeling through my system. "Cam, that's just not good enough."

"Meg, honestly, why do you say that?"

I look at him, then look away. Force myself to meet his eyes again. "You just don't understand."

"What do I not understand? Tell me. I'm listening. Hang on ..." The line of cars in front of us is moving. "Let me load us on the ferry and then we've got the entire ride over for you to explain this to me."

As soon as we're parked, with the attendant inching us forward into bumper-to-bumper proximity with the car in front of us, Cam cuts the engine and says. "Shoot. I'm listening."

I pick up my now-useless list and fold and unfold it, and try to figure out where to start. "It's been a long time since you've lived with them, Cam, but it's important to them – to Mom – that things are right."

"You think I don't know that?"

"This weekend, in particular, I overheard her talking to Dad and laying it out, detail by detail, the way she wanted the dinner to be – turkey and all the trimmings – and that's what she's going to expect, Cam."

"Meg, is that what you want?"

"What do you mean?"

"Do you want to sweat the small stuff like that? To that level? Sometimes you have to just let things go."

"But, Cam ..." I'm not explaining myself properly. "Here's the thing with Mom and Dad. You scratch their back, they'll scratch yours. We give them what they want; they'll be on your side ..."

"What, exactly, are you worried about?"

"I'm worried they're going to come down hard on you. I'm worried you've helped me get Major and now you're going to get shafted and not get to go to Montreal."

I wait for Cam to laugh at me, or snort at me – clearly he doesn't remember just how particular my mother can be – but instead he just puts his hand on my shoulder. "Meg. You're going to drive yourself crazy worrying about stuff like this. I'm going to Montreal, one way or another. I've already decided that. And if one dinner changes Mom and Dad's mind about supporting me, so be it."

I open my mouth to protest, and he cuts me off. "Also, I think you're not being completely fair to Mom and Dad. I mean, sure, they have high expectations and, yes, Mom in particular can be a bit over-the-top, but they're not completely unreasonable. I mean, *they* were the ones who both worked today. If anything they should feel guilty about abandoning their children on Thanksgiving weekend." He pauses, then adds, "And there's nothing we can do at this point anyway, so I think you're just going to have to trust me."

I look down at my list, with the paper gone slightly furry from over-handling. The word "turkey" pops into view and, triggers a lightbulb in my brain.

I bounce in my seat and say, "Actually, I might not have to. There might be something we can do after all."

"What are you talking about?" Cam asks.

I push the car door open. "Just give me a few minutes. I have to double-check something. I'll be back."

The wind whips through my hair and the thick clouds that have closed in to cover the sun mean there's nothing to counter the chill of the gust off the lake. That's OK. I'm not planning to hang around on the deck anyway.

I have to push hard to break the vacuum created by the wind against the passenger lounge door, but it gives and spills me into fluorescent lights and a warmth in such contrast to outside it burns my cold cheeks.

Most everyone seems to have stayed in their cars. There are a few people scattered across the benches. One scrolls through something on her phone. Another reads a book. A third pages through the free local newspaper.

Nobody's at the bulletin board – nobody's in my way. I step over to the board, afraid to breathe in case I'm wrong, and hunt for the paper I'm picturing. *Green.* I'm sure it was that terrible pastel green colour schools, and churches, and other institutions tend to favour.

It had a turkey on it. A cartoon turkey. I think. If it's here. If I wasn't imagining it.

I catch sight of a sliver of green peeking out from behind a notice of a house for rent and There. It. Is.

Oh my ...

Old Fashioned Home Cooked Turkey Dinner it says. With all the trimmings it assures me.

At the church hall, today from 4:30 p.m. to 7:00 p.m. Adults $15.

And then the most important thing of all: New this year. Avoid line-ups. Call in your take-out orders.

Take-out. Oh. My. Goodness.

We're saved. It's all good. We're fine.

My hand shakes as I take a picture of the poster and I'm so intent on getting back to my brother that when I, quite literally, run into a ferry hand, I nearly forget to hand him the high visibility jacket I have slung over my arm.

Chapter
Twenty-One

I wasn't ready to believe it. Couldn't let myself relax. Stood in line to pay for our take-out dinners with fingers on both my hands crossed yet again.

But now I've handed over my dad's twenty-dollar bills, and received four generous-sized styrofoam containers in return and my brother and I are going to put a full turkey dinner on the table.

Problem solved.

Except, since Cam's gone to return Ty's car, we still need to cycle home. The mercury's plummeted and I'm trying to pretend I didn't see three or four random snowflakes twirling through the air on the way here.

Whatever. It doesn't matter. We won't freeze on a 10K bike ride. We'll just pedal fast. We'll have to so we can keep a decent lead on my parents who, even though they're a ferry ride behind us, will zip along the highway once they get off the boat.

I stand in the doorway of the church hall with a plastic bag dangling from each hand and once again I'm muttering under my breath, *"Where is my brother?"*

After taking Ty's car back he was supposed to grab the bikes and wheel them up here to meet me. We were going for efficiency, for time-saving.

"Fine," he said. "If it's so important to you, I'll help you. After all, this is a pretty awesome solution to the dinner situation."

Which sounded promising, but now I'm ready to go and he's nowhere in sight.

"Cam ..." I readjust the handles of the bags. "Cam!"

"Yes?"

He's coming around the corner. He's wheeling both bikes.

"Oh, thank God you're here. Let's go!"

I hand him one of the bags. "These ones are Mom and Dad's so be careful! Wait ... why do you already have a bag? What's in it?"

He's already on his bike, already pointing it down the slight dip toward the road. He calls back over his shoulder. "Tell you at the cottage!"

I have to hustle to swing my leg over the cross bar of my bike, arrange my plastic bag where it won't interfere with my brakes, and pedal like crazy to catch up to my long-legged brother.

* * *

"I forgot about the wind!" It whips my words forward to my brother, who lifts his hand from the handlebars and shoots me a thumbs-up. The wind on this island can make-or-break your day and, right now, it's making ours. It roars behind us, shoving us forward; sometimes so quickly my feet can't pedal fast enough to keep up with my spinning wheels.

We make it to the cottage in record time and I sprint inside while Cam puts the bikes away.

I dump my coat on the floor, step out of my shoes and punch the numbers into the oven.

Then it's a quick search through the cupboards for oven-safe serving dishes. I open the four containers and scoop all the mashed potatoes into one dish, fork all the turkey into another, and put the vegetables in a third.

"There are dinner rolls!" I yell, wrapping them in foil.

"Pardon?" Cam asks.

"Dinner rolls. From the bakery."

A spatula gets every last drop of gravy out of styrofoam cups and into a saucepan, which goes covered on low on the stovetop, and I step back, take a deep breath and turn to watch my brother, setting the table with the good plates.

"Done!" I say.

"Good job." He looks at his watch. "Now we have a few minutes to cover our tracks."

"What do you want me to do?"

"First of all put your coat away because, of course, you've been home all this time, haven't you? Then, wash those containers and I'll take them straight out and hide them at the bottom of the recycling. And, finally, this!" He holds up the bag he was carrying in the village.

"Yeah, what is that?"

"If we're going to do this, we're going to do it right." He grins – "Voila!" – then hands the bag to me and I peer inside to see ...

"Yuck!"

"But brilliant, right?"

I sigh. "Yes, OK, OK, you're brilliant."

The bag is full of bones. Turkey bones. And skin. Some potato and carrot peels, too. "Where did you get this?"

He reaches under the sink and hands me the small compost container we keep there. "Garbage cans behind the church."

I upend the contents into the mini-composter and Cam yelps. "Look!" He fishes out a wishbone and sets it on the windowsill the way my mom always does, so it can dry and we can make a wish. "The final touch of authenticity."

"Not bad ..." Out of the kitchen window a flash of movement catches my eye. "A car!" I point. "Just taking the corner." I hand the piled-together containers to my brother. "Hurry, hurry, hurry!"

As the door closes behind him I take two seconds to turn in a slow circle, surveying the table, the oven, and the heaped composter left out on the counter.

I take a step forward, dip a spoon into the gravy, dribble a couple of drops on the burner, and put the lid back on.

There. That's the best we can do.

Chapter
Twenty-Two

"This is lovely."

I don't always agree with my mom, but right now I do.

Especially because they used their unexpected extra time waiting for the next ferry to find a bakery that was open despite the holiday, and buy a cranberry pie.

It's truly delicious.

And we're eating it in a warm room, at a table strewn with the remnants of a good meal – those church ladies know how to cook a turkey dinner – with the curtains drawn tight against the cold, dark night.

As much as I love the island and its views, the nights here can be deep and, sometimes, spooky. Especially during the colder months, there's nothing better than sitting in a room with folds of thick fabric keeping the dim, golden light in, giving a quality of cozy comfort to the cottage.

My dad straightens in his chair and clears his throat. He lifts his wineglass. "I have to hand it to you two. Your mother and I had a few fraught moments today – especially when we didn't make it on the ferry ..."

My mom stirs, now, and interjects. "I swear, that RV got there after us. We should have ..."

"Emily." My dad gives her a look and she subsides. "The point is, getting here, finding this dinner ready, well, it made all the difference. Your mother and I thank you."

My mom lifts her own glass, leans to clink his, and says, "Yes, thank you." She sets her glass back down on the table. "To be honest, this is much more than I would have ever expected. I mostly wanted us all to be together and I thought we might have pizza – still warm if I was lucky."

My brother kicks me under the table.

"This is much, much nicer though and it definitely improves my mood after too much work and traveling."

I kick my brother back. Our eyes meet and we wink at each other.

"Now," my dad says. "Who wants tea? I'll put the kettle on."

***

It's like the old days we never had.

But it feels like we should have.

My parents in an armchair each. Cam, for some unknown reason stretched on the floor. And me, cross-legged on the sofa sipping peppermint tea and listening.

They're discussing a legal battle that's been in the news lately – the new government reversing a law, reversed by the old government, covering marine species at risk. Cam cares because of his research. My mom cares because of the legal arguments. My dad cares because of the politics. I don't really care, but I'm happy to observe.

"Now, Meg. About this horse. Finally, we get a chance to discuss him. How did it go?"

This is why I was happy to observe.

I pretend to have a mouthful of tea. I pretend it's hot and I have to swallow it carefully. I pretend I have a cramp in my leg. I pretend this is no big deal. "He was great to ride."

This woman came into our English class once – a local author – she talked to us about giving and accepting critique and, when she did, she went to the classroom door, and pulled it closed, and said, "I've tried to think of a more polite way to say this, but there's no other way that's so clear. You have to give people a shit sandwich."

"He was great to ride," was the first part of my shit sandwich to my mom.

Now comes the hard part; now I have to deliver the shit.

She's waiting. She must know it's coming. "Even though he didn't quite feel like the right horse for me ... but he's certainly impressive."

There. Sandwich finished. I should feel more relieved. I might, if I could have managed to come up with something better than, "didn't feel like quite the right horse for me." Seriously? All that time to think about it and that was the best I could do?

I'm waiting for my mom to call me out for the weakness of my argument, for it's irrationality.

Cam's the next one to talk, though. "Tell her the good news, Sis."

"The good news ..."

My mom raises one eyebrow – she can do it, too – "Yes, Meg. Tell me the good news."

There's a muffled noise from the corner of the room. I think my dad's laughing – or trying not to – I shoot him a glare with *Not helpful* written all over it.

"Well, the good news is, the right horse was there."

"Really?" My mom taps her fingernail on her mug of tea.

I clear my throat. Sit up as straight as I can on the somewhat saggy cottage couch. "Yes. Really. He ..." I think of launching into his vital stats – height, breed, potential – but those won't mean anything to my mom. Instead I say the only thing I think might work. "... he reminds me of Goody. The chestnut who didn't pass the vet check."

"Oh." The tapping stops. The lifted eyebrow comes into line with her other one. "He does?"

I nod. "He does. Only *more*."

Cam pipes up. "You should see her with this horse, Mom."

My mom's softness drops away as she focuses her gaze on my brother. "How would you know?"

He shrugs. "Slate told me when she dropped Meg off. Said Meg was really ga-ga."

"Hmm ..." my Mom says. "So, tell me more about this horse, Meg."

"OK." I start in on his height, breed, potential and jam my hand under my leg with my fingers crossed that she please, please for the sake of all that's good in the world, won't ask me his name. Not just yet, anyway.

* * *

With my parents installed downstairs, Cam moves up to the sleeping loft with me.

When I clomp back up the stairs from brushing my teeth he's sitting on the second-least lumpy of the twin beds – I got the best one last night – scrolling around his phone.

Except ... his phone is still in a bag in the garage in Kingston.

"Hey! What are you doing with my phone?"

"Just ... wait a sec, Sis. I'm almost done."

My reactions are quicker than his, though. I make a quick grab, score the phone, and read through a text message conversation that stretches back over the afternoon and evening. Come to think of it, I haven't seen my phone for a while ... There's I'm really glad I met you today, then The feeling's mutual, followed by Wondering if you'd like to have a drink one night? and Hmm ... your place, or mine? They're between my brother – well my phone used by my brother – and Heather.

"You did not!" I say.

Cam shrugs. "Why not? I'm interested in her – and I'm single now – and she's interested in me ..."

"Maybe she's interested in me," I say. "After all it's my phone."

Cam does the one-eyebrow thing. "Well, think what you like, but after driving around back country roads with her, I have reason to believe I'm the one she likes. Besides, you should be thanking me. Why do you think she called her friend to ask about the horse? She didn't do it when Slate asked, did she?"

"So, your charm is the secret weapon you deployed on my behalf?"

"I think of it more as dead sexiness than charm, and more of a super power than a secret weapon but, yeah, whatever you call it, it worked for you." He holds his hand out. "Come on, I've got to answer her – you know there's no telling when the text will actually go through – and we – *you* – need her to stay happy for when Mom and Dad decide they're ready to ask her to trailer that horse to you."

"You and I both know Dad has very little to do with it."

He winks. "True. You and I also both know you've very close to winning her over."

"I hope so." I hand him my phone. "Here. But no sexting. That would just be *ew*."

"'Night, Sis."

"'Night, Bro."

Chapter
Twenty-Three

The rest of Thanksgiving unfolds in the unhurried, non-commercial, most-beautiful-time-of-the-year way that makes it my favourite holiday.

By the time I get back from my run in the morning, my dad's made a breakfast not completely reliant on the wonders of boiling water. With ingredients brought from home – like eggs, and milk, and maple syrup – we're able to have pancakes. There's real orange juice, too. And bacon.

We walk, and walk, and walk – along the shore, picking up sticks and using them to stir up the cold water, skipping stones (Cam and my dad are endlessly competitive about their number of skips), and craning our heads back and up to watch wave after wave of geese travel by.

We tromp away from the river through the fields surrounding Betsy and Carl's house – sometimes the ground beneath our feet squishes with autumn-wet rain water, in other places our legs swish aside the stalks and husks of end-of-season vegetation.

When we hit the concession line we turn back toward our driveway. It rained overnight, and the top layer of the road is saturated. Cam and I giggle as our shoes pick up a layer of gravel suspended in clay. It turns our shoes as slippery as skates, and we take turns pushing one another along.

"If you fall you'll never get that out of your clothes," my mom warns. "And I definitely don't want it in the cottage." But she's smiling, so we just laugh and keep going.

It's on the way back down the driveway to the cottage that my mom moves up to my side. There's a strip of grass growing between the two dirt ruts, and every few steps I use the vegetation to try to wipe the coating of mud off the soles of my shoes.

"So," my mom says. "About this horse."

I forget about the mud. It'll wear off eventually. "Yes?"

"What are the next steps?"

"Pardon me?"

"Your dad and I talked about it last night – to be honest we weren't sure what we'd find when we arrived here yesterday – but you and your brother have reminded us you're perfectly capable of good judgment, and I guess that should hold for this horse-buying decision as well. You know more about riding than either of us ever will. I don't like it when my clients try to tell me how to apply the law, so I guess I should let you make horse-related decisions."

"I ... wow ... I didn't think ..."

"Also, Meg, I know you think I'm all about facts, and figures, and evidence – and I do value those things – but I saw what you went through when you lost that other horse. It broke my heart – even if I didn't show it – and if this new horse can make that better, then, well, like I say, what are the next steps?"

"Alright," I say. "Well ..."

* * *

Leaving is sad, and great.

The island has a way of getting under my skin, into my lungs, of changing the rhythm of my life. I sometimes forget I miss it, until I'm here, and then I know there's been a hole in my life I've been too busy to notice.

We pull up into line and my dad shuts off the ignition, and when I squint toward the horizon into the low, late-afternoon sun I can make out the shape of the ferry coming in, and this is the great part of going. Because Major's over there. Craig wants to look at a large pony Heather has for sale, so she's trailering both of them to Craig's the day after tomorrow.

The day after tomorrow.

When I get home I'm doing all my homework. I'm going to work ahead. I'm going to make sure there's no competition for my time once Major arrives.

After lunch my parents talked to Cam about Montreal. They had questions. I pretended to read while he answered them. He did a good job.

They didn't offer to drive him there to look for an apartment, but they didn't flat-out say no, either.

My money would be on him convincing them.

There's just one little problem though. On our way home they want to drop him off at his house. Which, of course, is now Lauren's house.

Cam and I leave our bags in the car and go to the ferry dock to wait. "What are you going to do?" I ask.

"I'll figure it out."

"In the next twenty minutes?"

He puts his arm across my shoulder and gives it a squeeze. "Have you learned nothing this weekend?"

I let my weight fall against him. "I might have learned one or two things."

"It was fun," he says.

"Yeah, it was."

The boat comes in and we walk on.

"In, or up?" Cam asks.

The temperature has already retreated from its warmest point, and that wasn't too far into double digits. And, no doubt it'll be cooler as we cross the open water and the wind picks up.

But ...

We won't be back here again this year. And, as the sun sinks, its fiery colours inject a fierce beauty to the evening.

It'll be worth a shiver or two to stand on the upper deck.

"Up," I say. "At least until I freeze."

"'Kay. I'll meet you there. Just going to hit the washroom."

I climb the honeycombed metal stairs, the edges so sharp I can feel them even through the rubber soles of my boots.

At the top I pause and look down. Catch my parents' eyes through the windshield of the car. My dad waves, my mom bundles her arms tightly around herself and mouths, 'Brr ...' Yeah, *brr*, but beautiful.

I move to the outer railing, lean against it and turn my face into the dying blaze of the sun. Close my eyes. Bright as it is, there's not much warmth left in it.

When I open my eyes again, I can only see in two shades. There's light, and dark.

A ways down the railing a figure has appeared.

Slight, but fit. I can't make out details but I have a vague impression of work boots, jeans, a casual shirt. A baseball cap. I couldn't swear to it in court, but I'd say his hair has a wave to it.

What is strong, is this feeling I have. Joy, or something like it, bubbling through me.

It's Major being mine. It's Cam and I understanding each other. It's being on good terms with my parents. It's this place – the beauty and peace of it.

I tell myself it's all these things but something in me is telling me it's him, too.

It can't be. That's just silly.

He nods and I want to believe the nod is to me.

"What's the big smile for, Sis?"

A-a-nd, my brother's back. "Hey," I say. I'm still thinking of the guy. I blink to try to see him better but all I get is his back view, heading for the stairs at the other end.

My eyes have adjusted enough to tell me I like the fit of his jeans.

Cam snaps his fingers in front of me. "Earth to Meg. What's up?"

I give my head a shake. "So, have you figured out your problem yet?"

Cam grins, lifts his bag which he has slung over his shoulder. "Sure did. I'm getting a ride."

"Who with?"

"As far as Mom and Dad know, with a good friend. Which is kind of true, because this guy's saving my butt, so I count him as a good friend."

"What guy?"

"I ran into him down below. I was asking one of the guys who works on the ferry if they knew anyone who could give me a lift to the university, and this guy was walking by and said he would ... in fact, that's him, down there."

My brother points to a pick-up truck. I can't see the whole thing – it's partly blocked by a big livestock trailer, but I can see a guy climbing in. Baseball cap, jeans, work boots.

"Oh!" I say.

"What?"

"Nothing. Just, that's nice of him."

"World's full of nice people, Sis." I guess he's right. Maybe that was the vibe I was getting off the guy. A nice guy, helping my brother.

I have this unreasonable, yet overwhelming urge to get my bag, too, and go with my brother. I'm not ready to let go of this new friendship we've developed. Also, for some reason, I want to get to know baseball-cap-guy better – or, at least have the chance to say hi to him.

But ... mustn't be greedy. Everything's clicked for me over the last couple of days. How much more can one person ask for?

I hug Cam. "I hope you like your new apartment, and I hope the next time I see you you're on your way to Montreal."

"I will be," he says. "One way or another I'll figure it out."

"And thanks, Cam. Really. I owe you."

"Just enjoy the horse," he says. "Enjoy life."

"Will do."

I follow him down the stairs and, even though it's more than *brr*, I take an extra few seconds to stand beside my parents' car and watch my brother weave through the parked vehicles, heading for the baseball-cap-guy and his pick-up truck.

I'll see him again soon. And maybe not just my brother. It's a small island.

I pull the back door open, drop into the much-warmer car, and say, "Hey guys. I'm here. Ready to head home."

PLEASE LEAVE A REVIEW!

REVIEWS help me sell books. More sales let me write more books. A simple star rating and a few quick words are all that's needed to help other readers decide if they want to read my books.

To review, please follow this link – https://tinyurl.com/reviewSMH – and select your preferred retailer. Or, use this QR code:

If you liked this book ...

... you might enjoy Tudor's other books. Read the first chapter of Appaloosa Summer, Book One in the Island Series, to find out.

Chapter One

Appaloosa Summer • Island Series
Book One

I'm staring down a line of jumps that should scare my brand-new show breeches right off me.

But it doesn't. Major and I know our jobs here. His is to read the combination, determine the perfect take-off spot, and adjust his stride accordingly. Mine is to stay out of his way and let him jump.

We hit the first jump just right. He clears it with an effortless arc, and all I have to do is go through my mental checklist. Heels down. Back straight. Follow his mouth.

"Good boy, Major." One ear flicks halfway back to acknowledge my comment, but not enough to make him lose focus. A strong, easy stride to jump two, and he's up, working for both of us, holding me perfectly balanced as we fly through the air.

He lands with extra momentum; normal at the end of a long, straight line. He self-corrects, shifting his weight back over his hocks. Next will come the surge from his muscled hind end; powering us both up, and over, the final tall vertical.

It doesn't come, though. How can it not? "Come on!" I cluck, scuff my heels along his side. No response from my rock-solid jumper.

The rails are right in front of us, but I have no horsepower – nothing – under me. By the time I think of going for my stick, it's too late. We slam into several closely spaced rails topping a solid gate. Oh God. Oh no. Be ready, be ready, be ready. But how? There's no good way. There are poles everywhere, and leather tangling, and dirt. In my eyes, in my nose, in my mouth.

There's no sound from my horse. Is he as winded as me? I can't speak, or yell, or scream. Major? Is that him on my leg? Is that why it's numb? People come, kneel around me. I can't see past them. I can't sit up. My ears rush and my head spins. I'm going to throw up. "I'm going to ..."

***

I flush the toilet. Swish out my mouth. Avoid looking in the mirror. Light hurts, my reflection hurts, everything hurts at this point in the afternoon, when the headache builds to its peak.

Why me?

I've never lost anybody close to me. My grandpa died before I was born, and my widowed grandma's still going strong at ninety-four. She has an eighty-nine-year-old boyfriend. They go to the racetrack; play the slots.

If I had to predict who would die first in my life, I would never, in a million years, have guessed it would be my fit, young, strong thoroughbred.

Never.

But he did.

Thinking about it just sharpens the headache, so I press a towel against my face, blink into the soft fluffiness.

"Are you OK?" Slate's voice comes through the door. With my mom and dad at work, Slate's been the one to spend the last three days distracting me when I'm awake, and waking me up whenever I get into a sound sleep. Or that's what it feels like.

"Fine." I push the bathroom door open.

"Puke?"

I nod. Stupid move. It hurts. Whisper instead. "Yes."

"Well, that's a big improvement. Just the once today."

She follows me back to my room. She's not a pillow-plumper or quilt-smoother – I have to struggle into my rumpled bed – but it's nice to have her around. "I'm glad you're here, Slatey." I sniffle, and taste salt in the back of my throat.

I'm close to tears all the time these days. "Normal," the doctor said. Apparently, tears aren't unreasonable after suffering a knock to the head hard enough to split my helmet in two, with my horse dropping stone cold dead underneath me in the show ring. I'm still sick of crying, though. And puking, too.

"Don't be stupid, Meg; being here is heaven. My mom and Agate are going completely over the top organizing Aggie's sweet sixteen. There are party planning boards everywhere, and her dance friends are always over giggling about it too."

"Just as long as it's not about me. I don't want to owe you."

"'Course not; you're not that great of a best friend."

* * *

The way I know I've fallen asleep again, is that Slate is shaking me awake. Again.

"Huh?" I open one eye. Squinting. The sunlight doesn't hurt. In fact, it feels kind of nice. I open both eyes.

"Craig's here."

I struggle to get my elbows under me, and the shot of pain to my head tells me I've moved too fast.

"Craig?"

She's nodding, eyes wide.

"Like our Craig?"

"Uh-huh."

First my mom canceled her business trip scheduled for the day after the accident; now our eighty-dollar-an-hour, Level Three riding coach is at my house. "Are you sure I'm not dying, and you just haven't told me?"

"I was wondering the same thing."

"What am I wearing?" I blink at cropped yoga pants and a t-shirt I got in a 10K race pack. It doesn't really matter – I've never seen Craig when I'm not wearing breeches and boots; never seen, or even imagined him in the city – changing clothes is hardly going to make a difference.

Slate leads the way down the stairs, through the hallway and into the kitchen, where Craig's shifting from foot to foot, reading the calendar on the fridge. He must be bored if he wants the details of my dad's Open Houses, my mom's travel itinerary.

"Smoking," Slate whispers just before Craig turns to me. And, technically, she's right. His eyes are just the right shade of emerald, surrounded by lashes long enough to be appealing, while stopping short of girly. His cheekbones are high and pronounced, just like his jawbone. And his broad, tan shoulders, and the narrow hips holding up his broken-in jeans are the natural trademarks of somebody who works hard – mostly outside – for a living.

But he's our riding coach. Craig, and our fifty-five-year-old obese vice-principal (with halitosis), are the two men in the world Slate won't flirt with. I don't flirt with him, mostly because I've never met a guy I like more than my horse. Major ...

"Hey Meg." Craig's quiet voice is a first. The gentle hug. He steps back, eyes searching my head. "Do you have a bump?"

I take a deep breath and throw my shoulders back. "Nope." Knock my knuckles on my temple. "All the damage is internal."

Craig's brow furrows. "Meg, you can tell me how you really feel." No I can't. Of course I can't. Even if I could explain the emptiness of losing my three-hour-a-day, seven-day-a-week companion, the guilt at "saving" him from the racetrack only to kill him in the jumper ring, and the take-it-or-leave-it feeling I have about showing again, none of that is conversation for a sunny spring-time afternoon.

Still, I can offer a bit of show and tell. "I have tonnes of bruises. And I've puked every day so far. And, this is weird but, look." I use my index finger to push my earlobe forward. "My earring caught on something and tore right through."

The colour drains from Craig's face, and now I think he might puke.

"Meg!" Slate pokes me in the back. "Sit down with Craig and I'll make tea."

Craig pulls something out of his pocket, places it on the table. A brass plate reading Major. The one from his stall door. "We have the rest of his things in the tack room. We put them all together for you."

Yeah, because you wanted to rent out the stall. I can't blame him. There's a massive waiting list to train with Craig. And my horse had the consideration to die right at the beginning of the show season. Some new boarder had her summer dream come true.

I reach out; turn the plaque around to face me. Craig's trained me too well – tears in one of his lessons result in a dismissal from the ring – so now, even with a concussion, I can't cry in front of him. Deep breath. I rub my thumb over the engraved letters M-A-J-O-R. "There was nothing that horse couldn't do."

Craig sighs. "You're right. He was one in a million. Have you thought about replacing him?"

If you liked the first chapter of Appaloosa Summer, why not read the rest of the book? You can find it using this QR code.

ABOUT THE AUTHOR

TUDOR ROBINS is the author of books that move your heart, mind, and pulse.

A little piece of Tudor's own heart is in many places: the central-Ottawa neighborhood where she lives, the Gatineau hills and Eastern Ontario countryside where she loves to hike, Wolfe Island and the St. Lawrence River where she loves swimming and paddleboarding, and the university towns that are currently home to her children.

When she's not writing, Tudor rides, runs, quilts, and walks with her best friends and her Jack Russell / Potcake mix, Cara.

Please contact Tudor at tudorrobins@gmail.com!

Made in the USA
Las Vegas, NV
18 July 2022